MACKENZIE McKADE

A TALL DARK COWBOY

ELLORA'S CAVE
ROMANTICA PUBLISHING

*W*hat the critics are saying...

ॐ

5 Angels "Mackenzie McKade has created another fantastic story that totally pulls you into the world she has created. A Tall, Dark Cowboy is most definitely a Recommended Read." ~ *Fallen Angels*

5 Flags "Mackenzie McKade's A Tall Dark Cowboy is a fantastic read. I never wanted this book to end. I was laughing and crying until the very end. This well-written book is a romantic's dream. The powerful emotions the characters feel spill from the pages into the heart of the reader. Wyatt is a strong rugged cowboy willing to standby the people he loves no matter what. Lacy is an independent woman facing many obstacles in her life. The courage and grace she displays endears the character to the reader...I am looking forward to her next book." ~ *Erotic Escapades*

5 Hearts "This author's erotic voice is heavenly. If you love cowboys, sexy characters, emotional wealth and a novel written book, Ms. McKade cannot be beat! Lasso your copy today of A Tall, Dark Cowboy by Mackenzie McKade. It is available only through the number one publisher of romantica world wide – Ellora's Cave." ~ *LoveRomance*

5 Hearts "This is one of the most heartrending novels; so intense, so real. I found the absolute love that Wyatt has for Lacy, and her daughter so moving; so wonderful. The feeling comes through very well in the story of the magnetic pull between the two... they truly can't keep away from the other; so sensual, so warm. Definitely a man to keep. Put this right on your ToBeBought listing." ~ *The Romance Studio*

5 Stars "Mackenzie McKade takes the reader on a ride as thrilling as a rodeo. Lacy and Wyatt have preconceived ideas of who the other is. They are both wrong. No matter how hard they fight it, they are destined to spend their lives together...The sex between Lacy and Wyatt has the heat of a five-alarm fire. I cannot wait for Ms. McKade's next book." ~ *Ecataromance*

"A TALL DARK COWBOY is an emotional roller coaster. It will have you sweating one moment, in tears another, and laughing the next. Mackenzie McKade has done a truly wonderful job of creating characters that the reader will fall in love with and care for. The story will linger in your mind long after you have finished reading it." ~ *Romance Reviews Today*

4 Cups "I wanted this cowboy for myself! This was a great, hot love story to read. I was entertained by colorful characters all through this story. A great read to add to your collection." ~ *CoffeeTimeRomance*

"A Tall Dark Cowboy is a must read. A MUST read! The more Mackenzie McKade writes the better she gets, and A Tall Dark Cowboy shows her writing talent from beginning to end. I could not put this book down until I finished. Then, I found myself going back and picking it up again, just in case I missed something. It goes without saying that I highly recommend this book. Whether you are a fan of westerns or not, A Tall Dark Cowboy will make you tingle. Excellent job, Ms. McKade!" ~ *Joyfully Reviewed*

An Ellora's Cave Romantica Publication

www.ellorascave.com

A Tall, Dark Cowboy

ISBN 141995590X, 9781419955907
ALL RIGHTS RESERVED.
A Tall, Dark Cowboy Copyright © 2006 Mackenzie McKade
Edited by Heather Osborn
Cover art by Syneca

Electronic book Publication February 2006
Trade paperback Publication November 2006

Content Advisory:

S – ENSUOUS
E – ROTIC
X – TREME

Ellora's Cave Publishing offers three levels of Romantica™ reading entertainment: S (S-ensuous), E (E-rotic), and X (X-treme).

The following material contains graphic sexual content meant for mature readers. This story has been rated E–rotic.

S-*ensuous* love scenes are explicit and leave nothing to the imagination.

E-*rotic* love scenes are explicit, leave nothing to the imagination, and are high in volume per the overall word count. E-rated titles might contain material that some readers find objectionable—in other words, almost anything goes, sexually. E-rated titles are the most graphic titles we carry in terms of both sexual language and descriptiveness in these works of literature.

X-*treme* titles differ from E-rated titles only in plot premise and storyline execution. Stories designated with the letter X tend to contain difficult or controversial subject matter not for the faint of heart.

Also by Mackenzie McKade

ഇ

A Very Faery Christmas
Forbidden Fruit
Kalina's Discovery *(with Cheyenne McCray)*
Lord Kir of Oz *(with Cheyenne McCray)*
The Charade
The Game

About the Author

ഇ

A taste of the erotic, a measure of daring and a hint of laughter describe Mackenzie McKade's novels. She sizzles the pages with scorching sex, fantasy and deep emotion that will touch you and keep you immersed until the end. Whether her stories are contemporaries, futuristics or fantasies, this Arizona native thrives on giving you the ultimate erotic adventure.

When not traveling through her vivid imagination, she's spending time with three beautiful daughters, two devilishly handsome grandsons, and the man of her dreams. She loves to write, enjoys reading, and can't wait 'til summer. Boating and jet skiing are top on her list of activities. Add to that laughter and if mischief is in order—Mackenzie's your gal!

Mackenzie welcomes comments from readers. You can find her website and email address on her author bio page at www.ellorascave.com.

Tell Us What You Think

We appreciate hearing reader opinions about our books.
You can email us at Comments@EllorasCave.com.

A TALL DARK COWBOY

᠍ജ

Dedication

❧

To the real cowboy in my life.
Bill, thank you for being my rock throughout the years.
Without your support, encouragement, and love I would
never have made it this far.

I love you.

Trademarks Acknowledgement

The author acknowledges the trademarked status and trademark owners of the following wordmarks mentioned in this work of fiction:

Baskin-Robbins: Baskin-Robbins Ice Cream Co.

Cardinals: B&B Holdings, Inc.

Chevy: General Motors Corp.

Coors: Coors Brewing Co.

Corvette: General Motors Corp.

Cuervo: Tequila Cuervo La Rojena, S.A. de C.V. Corp.

Denny's: DFO, Inc.

Ford Escort: Ford Motor Co.

Jack Daniels: Jack Daniel's Properties, Inc.

Jacuzzi: Jacuzzi, Inc.

JB's: JB's Restaurants, Inc.

Jeep Cherokee: DaimlerChrysler Corp.

Mack Truck: Mack Trucks, Inc.

McDonalds: McDonald's Corp.

Mustang: Ford Motor Co.

Proxima: InFocus Corp.

Shangri-La: Pearce Gourmet, Inc.

Spider: Fiat Auto Societa per Azioni

SpongeBob: Viacom International, Inc.

Stetson: John B. Stetson Co.

Wendy's: Oldemark LLC

Wheaties: General Mills

Wranglers: Wrangler Apparel Corp.

Chapter One

ဢ

The moment Lacy Mason walked out of the High Country bar's storeroom it felt as if she'd stepped off a cliff.

With her free hand she grasped the wall to steady herself, holding a twelve-pack of beer tight in her other as she stumbled over the raised threshold. When both feet touched solid ground her teeth clicked together, the slight movement jarring her as the cold, wet cans pressed against her chest.

Shit! Mesmerized by the stranger eight feet away, she'd tripped through the damned doorway. Embarrassment flushed her cheeks.

Sucking in a ragged breath, she fought to regain her composure even as the fine-looking cowboy leaned lazily against the bar and studied her like he owned her. Dark sensual hunger raked her body. His look was a predatory assessment, one that sent a shiver up her spine like a million dancing fingers.

Another misstep had her wondering whether the tightening of her nipples was due to the cowboy or the condensation from the twelve-pack that now dampened her shirt, causing the material to cling and outline the fullness of her breasts. She braved another step, this time more in control.

Damn, but the guy was gorgeous. His dusky blue eyes glittered in the bar's low lights. A hint of a grin began to tip the edges of his sensual lips.

Lacy's heart skipped a beat.

Through heavy lashes she scanned his imposing frame. *Oh my*. Black Stetson and boots, tight Wranglers wrapped around muscled thighs, and a package that would make any woman want to see what lay beneath all that sturdy denim.

The mere thought of unveiling him inch by tantalizing inch made Lacy wet her lips in anticipation. At the same time a surge of liquid desire moistened the pulse beating between her thighs.

The man looked good enough to eat...mmmm, *all* of him.

No, not again! This man was trouble, with a capital T. Lacy shook away the last lingering threads of insane lust fogging her mind. Her gaze darted away, avoiding those incredible eyes and that tantalizing body as she hurried behind the bar with the twelve-pack. Only problem was, it moved her closer to the dangerous-looking cowboy.

Damn if the man's spicy cologne didn't surround her like a pair of strong arms. Like a magnet, she felt the pull of desire low in her belly.

"Fight it," she grumbled, mentally brushing away the feeling.

No way in hell was she going to become involved with a cowboy again. She'd just pretend *this* cowboy didn't exist.

Lacy's open palm pounded hard on the tarnished bar top to gain her boss's attention.

The short, stodgy man glanced her way while blindly pouring Jack Daniels in a shot glass without spilling a drop.

In the mirror behind Larry, a reflection of the handsome cowboy taunted Lacy. Christmas lights twinkled softly around his profile, almost as if they were laughing at her.

"Here's the beer, Larry," Lacy murmured. "I'm working the bull. Call if you need me."

The man nodded as he moved on to pour three shots of Cuervo. Lacy caught a whiff of the potent scent. Her nose wrinkled.

Whew, that liquor could spin a head. And in her aroused state, she could stand a stiff one herself...a drink that was. At least for now.

Head held high, she walked from behind the bar as far around the tall, dark cowboy as she could. Still she felt his eyes on her as she headed for the arena.

A line had already begun to form as Lacy pulled out the chair and eased behind the controls. When the band took a break it was her turn to entertain the crowd. Wednesday was usually a slow night, but the upcoming rodeo held yearly in Gilbert, Arizona, had High Country rocking.

To warm up the masses, she switched the mechanical animal on and let it slowly sway up and down. Thick, gray mats surrounded the artificial beast, leaving plenty of distance between the bull and the walls.

Picking up speed, she spun the bull around and then flung it in the other direction. Roars of approval sprang from the crowd.

It was a wild bunch tonight. Wild nights were usually profitable. Even before the first ride several men crammed dollar bills in the tip jar that sat in front of her. She flashed them her sweetest smile as her first victim climbed aboard.

Dressed in a colorful western shirt and black jeans, the man was a typical bull rider, short and wiry. The fact was even more evident in the way he straddled the simulated bull and drew his crotch close to his hand. Out of habit he hit the bull-rope several times as if packing rosin, the sticky substance a rider used to secure his glove to the rope. Of course there wasn't any rosin on this simulated ride.

Lacy had to smile.

The cowboy tugged at the brim of his hat before he raised his hand indicating his readiness.

Lacy watched him with delight.

He was going down.

From a dark corner, Wyatt Anderson stood and observed the woman behind the controls. Golden highlights burnished the brunette hair twisted in a severe knot that gave no hint to its length or feel. Two yellow pencils jutted out from the bun. She dislodged a pencil, wrote something down, then jabbed it back into place.

Aloof, that's what she was. There was a haughtiness about her pretty features that was intriguing. He'd noticed her small tilted nose, high cheekbones, full sculpted lips and proud stance when she'd coolly observed him earlier. But now her face softened with an expression of pure sexual femininity. A sensuality that perfectly balanced the contours of her body, her mannerisms.

Tight red jeans embraced each curve as if the material was making love to her long legs. A black tank top covered her like a second skin, hiding firm breasts. Yet it was the hint of a red lacy bra peeking out from the tank that told him she longed to feel the touch of a man.

Earlier, he'd noticed she had refused the attentions of a young cowboy, making it perfectly clear she wasn't available or interested.

But now she caressed each man with a smile that made Wyatt reach down and adjust himself as he hardened.

Was she a cock-tease? Did she simply get off leading a man around the room by his dick?

"Nice ride," her sultry voice purred to the cowboy dusting himself off as he rose from the mat. The man smiled, squared his hat, and then walked over and crammed a five in the tip jar. Wyatt caught the gleam in her eyes as the money left the cowboy's hand.

"Money hungry." His low voice revealed his aversion.

"What? You say something?" The man beside him, Chance, was a childhood friend, and the only reason Wyatt was in this bar tonight. Several of their pals were in town to compete in the Gilbert Days rodeo held every December. Wyatt had entered the bareback riding and steer wrestling competition, a foolish act for a grown thirty-two-year-old.

"No, just mumbling," Wyatt responded, keeping the woman in his sights. She intrigued him, stirred his curiosity.

"She's something. Wouldn't mind havin' that filly's long legs wrapped around me tonight," Chance's slow southern drawl crooned. "Think she knows what she does to a man?"

"She knows," Wyatt stated matter-of-factly, as she flung a wannabe cowboy from the hunk of metal. Something about the sparkle in her eyes made him think she got a thrill sending men soaring onto their asses. Still, Wyatt had to admit he wouldn't mind a taste of her, either.

"Lacy, I've got a twenty if you'll ride." A tall, lanky cowboy leaning against the wall waved the bill in the air.

The woman adamantly shook her head. "No way, Sam."

"Lacy, here's my twenty." The man next to Sam held up a greenback before he elbowed his friend.

"Here's mine," stated another man from the crowd.

The woman's brows furrowed. She hesitated as if considering the cowboys' offers, before shaking her head, again.

Yeah, no doubt the barmaid was motivated by money — like most women.

Greed was a turnoff, but the fact was, Wyatt wouldn't mind watching her ride either. He stepped out of the shadows and pushed his way to the front. Chance followed.

From his pocket Wyatt extracted a hundred dollar bill and held it high in the air. "Here's another hundred." He paused for effect. "If my math's any good, that's $160. How about it, *Laaacy?*" He placed deliberate emphasis on her name as he wiggled the *dinero* invitingly.

Chance whacked him on the back and the crowd roared their approval.

Wyatt's words and the hundred dollar bill immediately caught the woman's attention. Obviously tempted, her tongue whipped across her bottom lip as if she could taste the money.

Then their eyes met, locked. An unexpected wave of desire hissed through his veins.

Wyatt shifted his hips. He muttered, "Down, boy," as her gaze brazenly caressed him.

Without breaking her fixed stare she called to the bouncer eyeing the crowd. "Mark, run the controls for me."

The big man nervously shifted his weight from one foot to another and glanced quickly over his shoulder toward their boss still tending bar. "You sure, Lacy? What about Larry?"

Liquid gold eyes never left Wyatt's as she nodded her assurance. Quietly, she rose from the chair and glided toward the bull. A lissome hop, then a long, shapely leg slipped over the bull. Her knees hugged the machine like a lover between her thighs.

Wyatt heard the males in the audience release a collective groan.

By the ease in which she mounted, she'd obviously done this before. It screamed from every inch of her posture. The slow tantalizing way she slid her body tight against her hand had every man in the place holding his breath, wishing he were the lucky bull beneath her.

Wyatt watched a couple of men rush to the tip jar and willingly relinquish their money, an encouragement for a good show.

Oh yeah, this woman knew what she was doing. With a graceful sweep, her left arm rose and the bull began to move.

The man at the controls knew what he was doing, as well, when the bull began a slow, sensual pace. The speed and motion of the ride was set to enhance the sultry movements of the woman's svelte body.

This lady rode for the crowd. She swayed in erotic seduction. Heavy eyelids dipped, adding to her racy performance.

All the while, the tip jar continued to hungrily consume the lusty men's money.

Was that a wink? Wyatt's hot gaze darted from the sexy woman to the man behind the controls.

The bouncer returned the rapid blink, and the bull sped up a notch. With the escalation of speed, so did the men's vulgar comments.

"Fuck it, baby, I mean *ride* it," one man chuckled from behind him.

Another man grabbed the nearest waitress and kissed the woman as if he was going to crawl down her throat.

A stocky bouncer dressed in a Cardinal's jersey jumped to the woman's assistance. There was a small skirmish, quickly brought under control.

Obviously, the heat in the bar had risen a degree or two, along with each man's animal hunger.

Wyatt swallowed hard. Blood pounded in his ears as it made a mad dash to his groin, filling his balls and cock to the bursting point. The ache behind his tight-fitting jeans was hard to ignore.

He wanted her.

Along with the realization was a streak of red-hot need that left him both shocked and aroused. Casual sex—a one-night stand with a stranger—was not his style. No, Wyatt hadn't just ridden into town. He chose his partners carefully, sensibly, guarding his health, heart and pocketbook.

Yet the proof of his desire sprang alive between his thighs. The compelling need he felt for this woman was something he had never experienced. He'd have her at any cost.

The bull spun around, then back again, a movement that should have yanked her body about, but instead exhibited her fluid mobility. The woman rode the thing as if she had been born on it.

The quick, jerky movements tore the pencils and the clasp from her hair, sending a tawny flow of silk through the air. As the bull went into a hard spin, men rose to their feet. The release of the long tresses whipping around her brought the crowd from a soft rumble to a turbulent roar.

"Goddammit!" barked the bartender as his short legs carried him hastily from behind the bar. "Mark! Stop! Lacy get your ass off that thing!" The man continued to mumble as the mechanical bull began to decelerate. With it, the woman's flowing movements became slow, calculated.

Even now, she held the audience in the palm of her hand as the group thundered for more.

Wyatt saw her clench her eyes closed, still caught in the spin. When she finally lifted her lids, she wavered slightly and dismounted.

"Damn woman," Larry muttered. "Happens every time she gets on that fucking thing." His voice rose. "Damn you, Lacy. Wanna bring the cops here again? Mark, keep her off it. I mean it!" One more breathy curse and then Larry stomped back behind the bar.

"She'll have everyone fucking on the floor before long." The angry man settled a wineglass a little too hard on the bar's surface. It shattered into a million pieces. "Dammit!" He glared down at the shards of glass and then carefully began to clean up.

When Wyatt turned his attention back to the woman, he found her directly in front of him. Her tongue slowly caressed her full bottom lip. Fire blazed in her eyes.

She plucked the hundred from his fingertips. "Thank you." A sharp pivot spun her about. On featherlight feet she moved across the floor to retrieve the rest of her winnings.

"Next rider," she called out over her shoulder, and slithered behind the controls.

"God almighty, Wyatt." Chance's throaty tone revealed how the woman's ride had affected him. "That was a hell of a ride." His friend's hand was wrapped around Wyatt's biceps as if to steady himself.

"Hell of a woman," whispered Wyatt beneath his breath. He eyed her appraisingly. "I'll be having me some of that before the night's over." He drew his black Stetson low over his eyes and grinned.

"Dream on, big boy." A hearty slap on the back rocked Wyatt. "Hey, wanna take a spin on the wild side? See if you can outdo her," Chance said.

"Nah."

"Afraid she'll outshine you, cowboy?" Chance teased, as another rider hit the mat with a resonant thud.

Wyatt's brows furrowed. He gave a low grunt.

"Come on," Chance urged.

Wyatt pushed up the brim of his hat with one finger and smiled. Lacy wouldn't know what hit her.

Chapter Two

ɕɔ

"Any more takers?" Lacy asked, while her gaze scanned the crowd. Tips were good tonight, thanks to the mysterious cowboy. She glanced in his direction, but once again, he had vanished.

"My turn." The whiskey-smooth voice played havoc with her senses. She felt each word slide seductively down her spine.

Slowly her head rose. Her gaze darted over her shoulder. He stood slightly behind her.

Lacy attempted to force a sound from her mouth, but nothing came out. Her voice had turned to dust. Dry mouthed, she nearly choked and swallowed her tongue.

God, he's gorgeous.

"I'll take that as a yes," he chuckled, then boldly approached the bull.

Lacy felt her stomach pitch like a wild rollercoaster ride.

Where was her bravado?

Snatched away by the confident man strolling across the mat like he owned the whole damn place.

There was power in the leg that swung over the hulk of steel. When his hand clutched the bull rope, she watched the tendons in his arms tighten, like the muscles that were now tensing low in her belly.

No way, nuh-uh! She wasn't going to fall for a good-for-nothing cowboy, *again.*

Been there, done that.

Yet the attraction between them crackled and hissed in the air like an Arizona monsoon sweeping across the land.

Lacy wanted to deny it, push it aside. But the animal magnetism she had felt only once before in her life was raging. And like the first time, which had ended in total disaster, this would be no different.

No. Thank you, no. There wouldn't be a *this* time, she promised herself as he raised his hand.

Aimlessly, she switched the bull to low and pondered her next move.

Okay, do I thrash him about and allow his friend to cart him off to the hospital?

That would take care of her immediate problem—this uncomfortable attraction going on inside her. She could take care of the fire burning low in her belly later.

Before closing time, she'd find the most unimposing man around, take him home and screw his eyes out. No attraction, no fuss, no commitment.

Yeah, right. Like I'd even go there.

"He don't look as good as you did on that thang." A deep southern twang came from behind her.

Lacy turned her gaze toward the laughing hazel eyes of the man who had stood beside the tall, dark cowboy. Where the other man was dark, his friend was light. Blond hair, six-two, his grin showing a mouthful of white teeth.

"I'm Chance, and if you don't rack it up a notch or two, Wyatt isn't going to be happy."

She returned a weak smile. "So, Wyatt wants a ride?"

"Oh yeah...he wants a *ride*." The man's words made her uneasy as she caught the hidden meaning behind them.

Without hesitation, Lacy twisted the dial up two notches. "Well, we don't want *Wyatt* to be disappointed."

One never knew what a wild animal would do, mechanical or not, especially with an aroused woman at the controls. The man before her was a professional, ready for the unexpected as his body moved fluently with the bull.

He was a large man. Hell, he had to be six-four, too large really to ride...a bull, anyway.

Lacy should've been able to unseat him instantly, but he held on. The only thing she succeeded in doing was driving her own desire into the danger zone. Her breasts felt heavy. Lightning zapped her nipples, sending aftershocks to her pussy, and she didn't even want to think about that ache. Lacy was so wet she was afraid she'd slide off the chair.

Dial up another notch.

Still, the man seemed indifferent to the intensity of the ride or its sudden shifts in movement.

Lacy pulled the bull to a dead stop and then jerked it alive again. She saved this trick for the experienced riders she wanted to meet the mat. Surprisingly, he stayed in the saddle, as if glued in place. A couple more tricks proved unsuccessful to dump the man.

A thunderclap of approval went through the crowd. He'd won. Admitting defeat, she drew the bull to a halt.

The edges of her mouth dipped down as she wagged her head with satisfaction. "Not bad, *cowboy*, not bad at all."

He glided off the bull like it was nothing, and approached her. And it wasn't just a walk—it was more of a bold, arrogant stride.

He was good...and he knew it.

A knot caught in Lacy's throat. Would he be as good in bed? Another wave of desire dampened her panties.

Her heartbeat stuttered when the cowboy bent low, bringing their heads side by side. With a deep breath she inhaled his scent, a wild combination of masculinity and spices.

"I can ride anything put between my legs," he whispered, drawing back so that their gazes met. There was a hint of humor and invitation in his sultry grin.

"Including me?" She froze as the words slipped from her mouth. She literally bit her tongue, tasting the pungent flavor of blood in her mouth.

Where the hell had that come from?

"*Yesss…*" His response sounded dangerously like the hiss of a rattlesnake coiled and ready to strike. "When do you get off…? Work, that is?" His eyes grew intense as he awaited her response. His hot breath brushed over her face, and all Lacy could think about was his lips pressed to hers.

Oh God, what had she done now? She had propositioned a cowboy. Broken rule number one—and surely she would pay dearly for the mistake. This man was a heady combination of muscle, erotic charm and trouble.

"Well?" His brows rose in question.

She looked at his black, wavy hair and could actually *feel* the cool silky strands slip through her trembling fingers. What would it feel like to have his hair resting on her thighs as he feasted between her legs?

"One. I-I get off at one." She couldn't stop the tremor in her voice.

Oh, this just kept getting better. Had she really just agreed to hook up with this man?

"I'll see you at one. Oh, by the way, my name's Wyatt."

She cleared her throat. "Lacy."

"I know," he flashed a warm smile her way, before his six-foot-four frame turned and headed for the bar.

Yep, she'd done it. Propositioned a stranger, and a cowboy at that. If she didn't think quickly she'd be in the man's arms by 1:15.

Her subconscious took the opportunity to wake up and casually ask, *And what would be so bad about that?*

Well, you know…he's a cowboy!

The soft buried voice responded, *You need this. He's a man first, cowboy second – who will be gone by Monday morning. Out of sight, out of mind. You don't want the complications of a relationship anyway. Jessie is your main concern.*

Okay, okay, I get your point. Still, Lacy felt an uneasiness creep across her heated skin. She must be crazy.

Clearly. You're talking to yourself, her inner voice chuckled.

Like a predator, Wyatt watched Lacy throughout the night. Every so often, he would catch her staring. As soon as their eyes met, she'd turn away.

Was she going to run, renege on their fantasy night? He couldn't let that happen. With each passing minute, she consumed his thoughts. He had to have her.

Just the thought of stripping her naked, feeling her soft skin against his and plunging between her thighs made Wyatt's cock harden with anticipation.

Laughter broke his reverie as several more acquaintances wandered in and joined him. He looked around and settled for a table near the band, which just happened to be in Lacy's section, where she was currently serving up a bunch of thirsty cowboys.

As she floated by, he caught the scent of her floral perfume, light and suggestive. He could watch her all night. The provocative sway of her hips and the daring cleft between her full breasts screamed sensuality and subtly promised a night of heaven in her arms.

Again, he pictured thrusting his cock between those long, slender legs—legs that would clutch him like she had that mechanical bull. No eight second ride for him. He planned to fuck her all night long.

"Have another." Gordon, a small wiry cowboy out of Lubbock, Texas, pushed the chilly beer Lacy placed on the table into Wyatt's hand.

"Nah." Wyatt set it back down choosing to nurse the longneck he already held. "I have plans tonight. Need to keep my wits about me." He smiled up at Lacy and then gave her a wink as she reached for an empty beer bottle. Her hand slipped and several bottles tumbled over as she dove to catch them.

"Here, little lady, let me help you," Gordon offered. With his overly enthusiastic assistance, she settled the empties on her tray and moved hastily from the table.

"Not much of a waitress, but a damn good looker." Gordon leaned into Wyatt. "Did you see those lips? Makes me hard…" He reached down cupping himself to verify the fact. "Yep, hard just thinking about them wrapped around my dick."

"Wyatt, here, gave her a hundred," Chance said.

A nasty little smirk overtook Gordon's lips. "What ya get in return?" Chair legs screeched across the wooden floor, as he scooted his seat closer, eager to hear all the sordid details.

"A ride," replied Chance, a mischievous grin pasted on his face.

"You're kidding, a lap dance?" Gordon's gaze followed Lacy's ass across the floor, then darted back to Wyatt. "You lucky prick."

"No, dickwad. Wyatt paid her to ride the mechanical bull." Chance motioned to the hunk of metal lying dormant behind them. "And, let me tell you, if she fucks *anything* like she rides, the man who takes her home is one lucky sonofabitch."

Wyatt inwardly smiled. Tonight he *was* that lucky sonofabitch.

As Lacy walked by, he wondered if her panties matched the red lace bra. Were they silky, a wisp of transparent lace or a racy thong? He looked absentmindedly at his watch. Two hours before discovery.

The man packed a hell of an erotic punch. Every time Lacy got within ten feet of him her knees weakened, her palms perspired. Like a lodestone, her body appeared drawn to his. If her traitorous body reacted to the mere presence of the man, what would it do when his hands caressed her?

She released an involuntary groan as her nipples puckered and her breasts grew heavy with anticipation.

"You okay, Lacy?" Mark asked, the bouncer's gaze following the path of her stare. He frowned, taking in the boisterous cowboys. "Something troubling you?"

"Nah, it's just been a long night." She glanced nervously at her wristwatch. *Two more hours*.

"Rowdy crowd."

"Yeah, it'll be like this until Monday. Damn rodeo. Damn cowboys!" she blurted, walking away in a huff.

* * * * *

The night was cool and crisp as Lacy punched the hospital number into her cell phone. She leaned against

27

someone's old 1969 Chevy truck, one boot propped behind her on the driver's side tire.

"St. Joseph's Hospital, Intensive Care, Pediatric Unit," a female voice answered.

Lacy pulled the thumbnail she'd been chewing from her mouth. "Can I speak with Nurse Bolton?"

"This is she."

"Nancy, this is Lariat, uh...Lacy Mason. How's Jessie?" Lacy clenched her teeth and her heart raced in her chest. She always braced herself to hear the worst, hoping for the best.

"She did well tonight. She's resting peacefully."

The weight of several hundred pounds of guilt seemed to float from Lacy's shoulders. "If she wakes, tell her that Mommy will be there first thing tomorrow morning."

"She's fine, Lacy. But if she wakes I'll let her know."

"Thank you." Lacy snapped the cell phone closed. Cradling the telephone tightly to her breast, she bit her lip to keep the tears at bay. She should be with her daughter. But they needed money. She had no choice.

Raised by her elderly grandmother, her parents taken in a car accident when she was five, Lacy had no one to count on but herself. And tonight that weight on her shoulders felt twice as heavy. Everything seemed to be closing in on her.

"I thought I saw you slip out the door." The velvet touch of Wyatt's voice flowed over Lacy and she startled, jerking her head up to see him in front of her. "Not running out on me?"

"Huh? No, no, I just had to make a telephone call." Lacy raised the cell phone as if to say, "See?" She attempted a smile but she knew it missed its mark when Wyatt frowned.

"Everything okay?" A warm hand grasped her elbow and then moved slowly up her bare arm to her shoulder. His thumb brushed gently across her skin.

Lacy trembled at his searing touch. A mixture of emotions hit her like a gust of wind. Fear, pain and yes, even desire struck hard, literally throwing her off balance. She stumbled as the cowboy caught her and drew her into his arms.

The compulsion to feel another's touch flowed through her. God, how she needed to be held, held in strong arms that would drive away the insecurities, the fear. And possibly, just for one night, satisfy the hunger that raged inside her.

Desperately, she clung to the comfort she gained from his embrace. All the while, he stood, unaware of the strength she stole from his caress.

"Lacy, you okay?" he asked again.

Shit! She released the death grip she had on him, tipped her head up and nodded just before his lips found hers.

The kiss was featherlight, soft, seeking. His tongue probed, urging her lips to part. When she opened for him, he slipped inside to taste her.

Goose bumps skittered across Lacy's arms. It was a gentle exploration of lips, teeth, every inch of her mouth.

Without thought, her arms locked around the man's neck, drawing him closer and deeper into the kiss.

Her aggression was like a switch that triggered his desire, intensifying it. In a heated rush, his hands began to roam until one traced a path beneath her breast. Her nipples tightened, stinging with desire.

Reality struck.

Lacy broke the kiss. Warmth spread across her face like wildfire. *God, he probably thinks I'm easy.*

Hell, yes, he thinks you are, her conscience cried. *How could he think otherwise? You nearly threw yourself at him, twice.*

Lacy fought for words that would save her some dignity, but they never came.

"Now, are you going to tell me what's wrong? What brought this on?" Wyatt stroked her back in small circular movements one would use to ease a child. "It's obvious you're upset."

Lacy stared at him dumbfounded. The man was insightful. Good looks and intelligence, too. A dangerous combination.

She tipped her chin and stared into his dusky blue eyes. "I-I need to get inside." She pushed from his arms, turned and all but ran back into the bar, leaving him alone in the parking lot.

Dark desperation had shadowed the woman's eyes when she pulled away from him. As he watched her hightail it back into the bar, Wyatt realized Lacy was an enigma. Daring and assured one moment, then almost childlike the next, as if something haunted her.

Retracing her steps, he entered the bar. He spotted Lacy taking an order from a couple seated at a table next to his. She glanced his way and then her gaze quickly darted away.

Chance sidled up to him as Wyatt took a seat. His friend waved at Lacy, catching her attention. His finger pointed to his beer and then made a circle indicating another round of drinks.

Chance's gaze followed Lacy as she picked up an empty beer bottle from an abandoned table. A sigh pushed from the man's mouth as he turned to face Wyatt. "Wyatt, we're going to JB's for breakfast. You gonna join us?"

"Nah, I've got plans," Wyatt responded. He watched Lacy's hips swing as she walked toward the bar. Man, she had a fine ass. She leaned across the bar to grab some napkins. The smirk on her boss's face as he snuck a peek down her blouse said the man thought she had a great rack as well.

"Plans?" Chance repeated as Lacy approached, tray full of another round of drinks.

A blush tinted Lacy's cheeks as she set down their order, gathered their empties and then glanced at Wyatt. Without a word she turned and stepped away.

Chance's gaze darted from Wyatt to Lacy, and then back at Wyatt. "You dirty dog." He slapped Wyatt on the back. "You're going home with that gorgeous waitress." He shook his head. "No wonder you haven't been interested with any of the tail panting over you tonight."

Wyatt simply smiled. It was ten to one and already he was playing out the fantasy he would enjoy with Lacy. How he would peel those jeans off her long legs. Roll her shirt up past full, firm breasts. Unveil her completely. His cock jerked and strained against his pants, begging to be released.

Wyatt shifted in his chair, adjusting his swelling erection. "Hold on, partner. It won't be long."

The uncertainty in Lacy's eyes said it all as she joined Wyatt after her shift. She was going to run.

31

"I need to wash the bar smell off me," she whispered for his ears only. "I'll give you my address and you can come over in say…about an hour."

Boy, was that the oldest trick in the book. Probably a fictitious address. He wasn't letting her off the hook that easily.

"How about I follow you home and wash your back," he spoke softly as his hands moved across her bare shoulders causing her to shiver.

Speechless, she nodded then headed for the exit. In silence, Wyatt followed Lacy out the door and into the parking lot.

Car and truck doors slammed as people prepared to leave. The heaving sounds of someone who had a little too much to drink came from behind a hedge, and laughter and song sprang from three women in a yellow Mustang convertible.

Lacy stopped in front of a car that had seen better days. "I live only a couple of miles south of here."

When she unlocked the vehicle, Wyatt held the door, blocking her way. With the back of his hand he caressed her cheek. A shadow crept across her eyes, confirming her uncertainty. He had to do something—anything—to take her mind off whether she was doing the right or wrong thing, so he pressed his lips to hers.

She melted against his body. The kiss was brief, just a sample, enough to wrench a smile from her taut lips.

He stepped aside and she climbed in. "I'll be right behind you." The car door slammed shut with a thud as he headed for his truck.

Still, the haunted look in her eyes ate at him as he followed her Ford Escort down one street and then another.

Hands thumping against the steering wheel to the tune on the radio, Wyatt had the uncontrollable urge to taste her, spread her wide and explore the depths of her body. A smile crept across his face. He wanted to hear her scream his name, beg him to take her, feel her warm, wet flesh around him.

His cock twitched with anticipation. Blood filled him to an aching hardness that had him shifting his hips to find relief.

With ease he followed her vehicle's bright taillights. Lacy didn't live far from the bar—she led him into an apartment complex two miles away. He pulled his truck up next to her car and turned the engine off. Country music continued to blare from his vehicle until he opened his door and stepped out.

He activated the self-locking feature of his vehicle and then turned toward her, stuffing the little black controller into his pocket.

"We're here." Her voice cracked with a hint of apprehension.

A heavy breath raised her breasts. He itched to take her into his arms and taste her, ease her fear. Yet, he was afraid if he touched her now she'd bolt and run. He'd broken many a skittish filly, and this one was no different. She needed a gentle touch, but also a firm hand.

In silence he followed her up a flight of stairs to the last door on the left. She fumbled in her purse, dropping the keys twice before successfully opening the door. Reaching into darkness, she snapped on the light and waved Wyatt in.

Wyatt's eyes scanned Lacy's small apartment. It was devoid of any knickknacks or other items women usually displayed to give a house that homey feel. In fact, it appeared as if she'd either just moved in or was preparing to move out. Several heavily taped brown boxes lay stacked in a corner. Only a worn leather loveseat, chair and coffee table adorned the room.

A small kitchen was separated from the living room by a breakfast bar. The pass-through revealed a wooden dinette set with two chairs pushed neatly beneath it.

"It's not much, but its home." Her voice held an air of apology.

"Looks great to me," he said, taking off his Stetson and placing it on the coffee table.

"Make yourself comfortable. There's beer and soda in the fridge, rum and whiskey above it. Glasses are in the cabinet to the right. I'll be just a minute." Then she turned and disappeared into the bedroom, the door slamming shut behind her.

Wyatt took another look around and then walked into the kitchen and opened the refrigerator. An untouched six-pack of Coors sat on the top rack. One soda was missing from a twelve-pack. Other than that, there wasn't much more inside, with the exception of a couple of yogurt containers, a single apple and a small pint of milk.

Guilt rode him for a moment. No wonder she was money hungry. She had nothing. Withdrawing his hand, he left the beer where it sat. He acknowledged that she wasn't the gold digger that he'd thought she was—that he'd judged her too harshly before getting to know her.

Fact was, a woman like Lacy shouldn't live like this. She should be draped in silk and diamonds living the easy life. He slowly closed the refrigerator and wandered back into the living room.

The creak of water pipes brought his attention to the bedroom. A grin crawled across his face. What did he have to lose? Either she'd welcome him or she'd toss him out on his ass. He decided to take a chance and headed for the door.

Now, this was more like it. His gaze scanned her bedroom. A thick, fluffy wine-colored comforter graced a queen-sized, four-poster bed piled with pillows of every shape, color and size. Her dresser was littered with female essentials—perfumes, glass trinkets and several pictures of a little girl, giving the room a lived-in and welcoming appearance.

It was a pleasant room, comforting, until he glanced at the red lacy panties and bra lying on the bed confirming his earlier suspicions. Not to mention the delicate, black silk negligee lying seductively across a chair. With one look, blood shot to his groin filling his cock to an aching tightness.

He moved to the bathroom door and began to undress.

Water fell in a brisk cadence over Lacy's tense shoulders, down her belly, rolling off her legs to puddle and then whirl, disappearing down the shower drain. The soothing warmth covered her like a blanket. The fresh scent of herbal shampoo filled her nose. She closed her eyes, threading fingers through her soapy hair. For a brief moment, she forgot about the man lingering in the living room.

Then the black negligee she had laid out flashed before her eyes and she cringed. No, she wouldn't wear the flimsy piece of temptation. Instead, she would dress in jeans and a t-shirt. What had she been thinking?

When the door of the shower opened, she startled.

Looked like she wouldn't need the jeans and t-shirt, or the negligee for that matter.

Chapter Three

ɞ

"May I join you?" Lacy heard his whiskey-smooth voice just as a dab of shampoo slipped into her wide eyes.

"Dammit!" she cursed, more frustrated that she missed a peek at his male nakedness than the sting that burned her eyes. Her trembling fingers rubbed at her clenched lids attempting to disperse the soap, only managing to make it worse.

"Here." He guided her hands away from her face and turned her toward the spray of water. "Try to open your eyes and let the water wash the soap out."

Standing behind her, he placed a hand on each side of her head and tilted it backwards. Lacy tried to blink, but was distracted by the gentle hands that began to rinse shampoo from her hair. His deft fingers glided easily as the water beat on her face.

His touch and the rush of water robbed Lacy of breath. Her mouth opened, catching a flow of liquid. She gasped— then choked.

A hushed chuckle escaped Wyatt's lips. "Here." He released her head, allowing it to fall slightly forward, which helped to shield her nose and mouth from the downpour. "I didn't mean to drown you. Can you see? Does it still hurt?" he asked, as strong hands slid down her arms leaving a path of searing heat in their wake.

Her eyes still burned a little but at that moment she didn't really care. "Yes—no. Thank you." Her heartbeat skipped a beat. Could he detect her nervousness? Could he tell how much she needed this, needed him?

"You're welcome, ma'am," he said in a low, southern drawl. "Always wanted to come to the aid of a naked damsel in distress."

His light teasing helped break the tense moment. Lacy released a giggle. "I never realized a cowboy could be so useful in a situation like this."

The fact that her bare body was pressed against a naked man was momentarily forgotten.

"Oh, I think I could amaze you." His warm breath teased the nape of her neck sending a shiver through her. "Shall I show you?"

With four simple words and the fact that his jutting erection slid easily between the cleft of her legs, Lacy's pulse took off as if it had just entered a horserace. And if he kept moving like that, back and forth, she was assured first place.

"Yes," Lacy said, breathless and without hesitation.

What the hell. Go for it! her conscience encouraged.

While the shower spray continued to beat down upon her, she awaited his next move. When soapy hands skimmed across her shoulders, then down her arms, her knees almost buckled. She watched in fascination as his long fingers slowly weaved through hers, massaging in and out, then disappeared to traveled up her arms until they reached her shoulders.

Lacy released a moan through clenched teeth as his hands glided down her back, pausing in that sensitive dip where her back ended and her ass began, before cupping the swell of her butt.

Her body felt like a furnace. She was burning from the inside out. With each gentle caress, he stoked the flame blazing through her veins.

Dry mouthed, she attempted to swallow but only managed to release another groan that urged his hands to seek more.

Sudsy fingertips made a path across her stomach, up her ribcage, until they reached her breasts, full and heavy with need.

When his fingers closed tightly over the taut peaks, she murmured, "Yes."

Tenderly he rolled the nubs between his forefingers and thumbs, then moved leisurely to stroke, pinch and caress.

Suddenly, his hands were gone and all that was left was the pounding spray of water. A cool breeze brushed between their heated bodies sending a chill through her, leaving her empty from the loss of his touch.

Lacy began to turn around, when she felt his now-lathered cock slide between her thighs. Thick, drawn-out thrusts teased her clit with slow, tantalizing strokes. The friction between her legs intensified as his weight drove her against the shower glass, flattening her breasts on the cold, hard surface as he continued to slip back and forth.

He grasped her wrists and held her hands above her head, palms flat on the glass as the warm water continued to stream over them.

"Oh God," she whispered, as shards of white-hot lightning burst between her thighs, filtering through her body. She needed his cock inside her, now.

Fingers interwoven with hers, he drove back and forth, continuing the blissful torment, stopping just before she grasped hold of the summit. He kissed her wet neck, her shoulders. His lips and hands danced across her skin, then his hips moved, stoking her desire anew.

Was the man trying to kill her?

"Feel good?" His voice was silk sliding over her body. His cock moved between her thighs with an increasingly steady rhythm. A sudsy delight she never wanted to end.

"Oh yes," she attempted to say, but her words came out a husky moan.

"More?"

"More." She arched her back, pushing the heat of her body against his thick erection encouragingly. The head of his cock nudged the opening of her pussy. "Just like that…" She tilted her hips, ready to take him deep.

A quick movement had her spun around and captured in his embrace. Their wet bodies melded together as his starving mouth came down upon hers in a wild frenzy of lips and teeth, sucking, licking, biting. The water continued to spray on their faces, adding to the eroticism of the moment.

Heat built, coiling low in her belly like a spring wound too tight. She needed his cock to mimic the sensual movements of his tongue mating with hers.

When he finally released her to take a breath, she stared into eyes dark with desire.

"Let's get out of here. I want to take you hard, fast. Then I'll make slow, passionate love to you for the rest of the night." His lust-laden voice revealed an urgency that promised a night of pure ecstasy.

Lacy's heart stopped. He wanted her as much as she wanted him.

In a whirlwind of fluffy towels, Lacy made a half-assed stab at drying her hair, but before she could wring the moisture from it, Wyatt scooped her up into his arms. His curly ebony chest hair was still damp as he pressed her to him.

Quick strides carried her toward the bed. She slid slowly down his firm body, feeling his thick erection press into her belly. His eyes were dark with passion.

The wait was over.

Then he frowned. Lacy felt her eyes widen as he stepped away and headed toward his clothing.

A moment of panic filled her. *No. No. No.* She was so damned horny and he was leaving? Without a word, the man was simply walking out on her. Hell, with a cowboy that usually didn't happen until *after* they fucked.

Her fists clenched. The heat of anger filled her cheeks as he bent, reached for his pants, and began to rummage through a pocket. Then relief filtered through her. He'd remembered the condom. In fact, there were several in his hands. Her heart fluttered as he ripped one of the small packets open with his mouth, and then began to slide the sheath over his engorged cock.

A growl came from somewhere deep in his throat as he padded across the floor, then set the remaining condoms on the nightstand. He took her firmly in his arms, meshing his mouth to hers. In a flurry of arms and legs they tumbled onto the bed.

His large hands were everywhere — seeking, touching, caressing. Her long, damp hair slid between their naked bodies as they rolled, her own hands grasping and feeling. She couldn't touch him fast enough — couldn't get him close enough.

It has been so long — too long.

She needed him inside her…*now.*

His body was solid muscle as he took control, positioning himself atop her. There was a pause when their eyes met. Stark hunger, raw and pure, raged white-hot like a flash of electricity.

He wasn't gentle. She didn't need him to be. Their teeth clashed, tongues dueled, but still it wasn't enough. Her nipples ached. Her pussy wept.

Now. She needed him to complete her body.

Her thighs quivered. Her legs parted, encouraging him to take more — take all of her.

It felt like she was caught in slow motion as their bodies came together, flesh to flesh, hips to hips.

Her fingertips dug into his back. She held her breath.

Pleasure raced through Wyatt like a lightning bolt as he pressed Lacy to him.

Her kiss was hungry, demanding, stirring his blood like no other woman ever had.

She wanted him. It screamed from every pore, from the way her body arched into his as if seeking to melt into him, to the dampness that welcomed his touch.

While his tongue searched the mysteries of her mouth, his fingers delved into the secrets lying between her thighs. She bucked against his hand, riding him hard.

Her short, fast breaths and soft moans drove him beyond control. He had to bury his cock in her hot, wet pussy soon or he was going to explode.

Lying on her back, her legs parted, inviting him into her. Before he realized it, his erection pushed past his hand, the head of his cock drowning in liquid delight as he plunged deep, impaling her with a single thrust that stretched and molded her around him. Her eyes closed. Her head lolled back as she cried out. The sound that pushed from her full lips was so profound, so passionate. He seated himself deeper inside her.

She was hotter, wetter and tighter than anything he could have imagined. It was like taking a nosedive straight into heaven.

Then the angel in his arms went wild.

Writhing beneath him, she locked her legs around him, lifting her hips to meet his every thrust. The soft whimpering sounds floating from her kiss-swollen lips made his blood heat.

Long fingernails bit into his back, trailing a burning path to his hips. She clutched his ass, driving him hard against her sex. Her body tensed, arched, and she released a scream of pure ecstasy.

Tremors shook her as a series of spasms milked his cock and squeezed out soft moans from somewhere deep in her throat. Her arms and legs clung to him almost desperately.

Wyatt couldn't hold back any longer. He attempted to withdraw before plunging for the last time, but she held on tight, refusing to release him. Her need was crushing as he ground his hips and pierced her hard, deep and fast. Eyes clenched, his back arched.

His climax was violent, an explosion that ripped from his body. It was a blaze of fire shooting down his cock, curling his toes as his sac pulsed, releasing his seed. His erection jerked several more times then stilled, filling him with a contentment he had never known.

As his pulse settled, he opened his eyes. Lacy lay quiet beneath him, sated delight softening her face. He felt a smile tug at his mouth, as he rolled to his side and gathered her into his arms. Like a kitten, she snuggled closer.

Lacy was everything Wyatt had expected, reacting sensually to his aggression. Her quiet moans excited him. Her screams made him crazy. She wasn't afraid to ask for what she wanted. Yet, it was her face, bright with passion, that made him feel every inch a man. She hungered for him.

Wyatt shifted his gaze to find her looking at him. He swallowed hard. No one had ever looked at him like that, with such intensity and heat.

But, there was something more. A desperation... A haunted expression he couldn't decipher.

"Wyatt, make love to me again." Her request almost sounded like a plea, filled with an emptiness that chilled him.

He wasn't ready for the tremor that shook him from head to toe. The despair in her voice was too much for him to deal with. He wanted her again, so badly that he felt his control slip. What was it about this woman?

"Give me a minute." He kissed the tip of her nose, and then rose from the bed, picked up a condom from the nightstand and headed for the bathroom. Disposing of the used condom, he washed and then slipped a new one on his already hard cock.

Entering the bedroom, he halted. His breath hitched. Lacy was sprawled across the bed. Her long, beautiful hair splayed over the pillow where she rested her head. A sheet draped her hips, but her breasts were exposed to his pleasure. She gifted him with a slow, sensual smile that put his feet in motion.

He might never learn what had caused her so much pain. But for the rest of the night he would do his best to chase the haunted expression from her eyes.

A sharp inhalation raised her breasts, the glorious peaks reacting, beading at his blatant stare. He had to taste them.

Without hesitation, he moved the sheet aside and parted her thighs, felt her warm, wet readiness against his palm. He ran his fingers through the dark curls at the apex of her sex before planting a kiss upon them, pausing briefly to inhale the heady scent of their lovemaking.

She trembled beneath his touch. Goose bumps rose across her belly as the stubble of his chin scraped along her skin. His lips feathered her body with soft kisses as he worked his way to her luscious breasts. Her thighs parted further and he pushed between them, his cock driving deep inside her.

Then his mouth closed on a delicious nipple. She arched into him, cradling his head, stroking his hair as he sucked her areola and fucked her beautiful pussy.

Once again, Lacy came alive in his embrace. His mouth met hers. She guided him onto his back, taking control, straddling and riding him, never breaking the sweet suction of their lips. Her needy hands caressed his body as his tongue stroked her hot, wet mouth.

When they parted she nipped and sucked and tasted his chin, his neck, the tight skin along his shoulders. She made him feel like she would die if she didn't sample and stroke every square inch of him.

She left no place untouched as she moved from his hips, her body releasing him. She slid down his thighs and took his cock between her lips.

Lacy cupped his balls, caressing them gently as her head bobbed. The cool, wet tresses of her long hair teased the inside of his thighs. He smelled the light aroma of the shampoo she used mingled with the heady scent of sex. He sucked in a tense breath. Through heavy lids Wyatt watched his cock slide in and out of the mouth he had just kissed. God, if only there wasn't a latex barrier between them.

Never had a woman affected him so deeply. Never had he felt another's passion as he did hers, as if she breathed his very essence inside her body. She left him confused. She left him breathless.

A shiver raked his spine. "Come here," he groaned, grasping her shoulders. "I want you to ride me like you did the bull tonight."

She smiled. "You do, do you?"

He nodded.

Like a siren, she crawled slowly, seductively atop him. Her long legs straddled him, her thighs exerting pressure against his waist. Using only her lower body, her hips dipped, catching his cock between her thighs and inhaling him in a single movement.

She was hot, wet as she began to move in long, drawn-out strokes that he felt pulling at the tip of his cock. She worked her vaginal muscles, squeezing him tightly, while her fingers brushed through his dark chest hair. Then she scraped her fingernails toward his bellybutton, causing a tremor that made her smile.

God, he loved it when she smiled. Her eyes laughed—sparkled—and no shadows lingered for the moment. He didn't understand why it mattered—it just did.

Bracing a hand on each side of her hips, he increased the pace, bringing her down hard. The sound of flesh slapping against flesh was heady music to his ears.

As he drove deep inside her he felt the back of her pussy pushing and rubbing against the small slit of his cock. His balls grew firm, his shaft lengthening with the rush of blood surging forward.

Lacy's features twisted as her climax shattered. Her eyes closed. She threw back her head and released a cry that broke on a ragged breath. She ground her hips into him as if wringing out every bit of sensation her body would allow.

Fingernails bit into his shoulders, the pleasure-pain pushing him over the edge.

It was difficult to decipher who groaned louder. Their bodies pressed tightly against one another. Together they fell into the abyss of ecstasy.

In the quiet that followed, Wyatt lay with a stranger in his arms. Yet he was more sated and content than he had ever felt before.

Golden brown strands of her silky hair slipped through his fingers. Like a child, she squirmed, wiggled next to him as she sought his body's warmth, comfort. Her simple movements made his cock twitch with another wave of desire.

In unison, Wyatt and Lacy looked down at his seemingly insatiable erection and laughter spilled from their lips.

"Down boy, she needs a rest," Wyatt chastised the body part continuing to grow in length and firmness. He shrugged. "Sometimes he just doesn't listen."

"Ummm…and I'm thankful he doesn't," Lacy cooed, as her hand gently embraced his member and began to stroke.

Tonight—or was it already tomorrow?—Lacy was going to take all that this handsome, willing man offered.

It had been so long since a man's hands had roamed her body, and never before with such sensual abandon.

So long since she'd allowed the worries of her daughter's condition to momentarily be pushed to the back of her mind.

Tonight was hers to enjoy. Tomorrow she would say goodbye, then pick up the pieces.

A deep, low growl brought her attention back to the appendage that she fondled in her hand.

"Come here," his voice was a gentle caress. His lids were half lowered, sleepy, sexy and more than she could resist as he handed her another condom. She didn't hesitate, slipping it over his rigid cock.

Powerful hands rolled her over on her back. Then he came down upon her. He closed his eyes and moaned in a way that reverberated through her. The slow, tantalizing strokes of his tongue across her neck, her chest, made her entire body jerk and quiver with each sensuous lick he delivered.

Lacy felt like an ice cream cone. His tongue lavished her neck and then slid down until his mouth found a nipple.

He bit.

Lacy squealed with surprise. His action sent tingles of fire shooting through her breast.

"You're a devil," she muttered, wanting, needing more of the sweet, sweet pain.

A lethal grin flashed for just a second. "Uh-huh," he replied, before adding, "Can I poke you with my pitchfork?"

Without waiting for a response, he buried his cock deep inside her, filling her completely.

"That feels so good," she blurted. A flush of heat consumed her face.

Deep-seated within her, he began to slowly pump in and out. "How about this?" his throaty voice hummed. His palms held him braced above her, so that she could see the playful desire in his eyes.

"Good," she responded. Her eyelids fluttered down and she took a deep breath.

Wickedly, he eased his cock out of her needy pussy. Her eyes sprang open. He stared down at her with one brow cocked. "Only good?"

Lacy grabbed at his hips. "Great! I mean great," she quickly corrected.

"That's what I thought." He thrust hard, causing her to gasp when his thick cock bounced off her cervix.

"More," she shuddered. He was so deep, filling her so completely.

"More?"

"More and harder," she moaned, her fingernails digging into his arms as her inner muscles clenched.

The slapping of his flesh striking hers was heady. He fucked her fast and he fucked her hard.

Her shallow pants quickened. She arched, her muscles and tendons tighter than a bowstring. Like an expert archer he plucked a delicate chord inside her and lights exploded behind her taut eyelids. A wave of heat shimmered through her as every muscle in her belly spasmed, clenching and releasing. One after another, white-hot fragments of electricity shot through her body, leaving the most delicious burning sensation. She jerked with each aftershock that racked her, until she heard Wyatt groan.

Lacy opened her eyes to see the expression upon Wyatt's face as his climax approached. It almost looked painful. Jaw clenched, eyes squeezed shut, he threw back his head and released a tortured sound that ripped from his throat as his body convulsed. Long moments later his head fell forward and he graced her with the most satisfied smile she had ever witnessed.

"Ahhh… Now that was great," he growled, before his elbows gave out and he rolled on his side. "Come here," he said and embraced her.

Cocooned in his arms, she sighed. No one had ever held her like this. So possessively. So completely.

Suddenly dread flooded Lacy with a vengeance. There was no relationship here. Tenderness? Yes. Sex? Hell yes. But love? No. It was a one-night stand, one-night rodeo performance, she reminded herself. In the morning he'd be gone from her bed, gone from her life.

A cowboy never stuck around.

Oh yeah, they came back for a quickie, played house occasionally, but they never made a home.

"You're trembling. Are you cold?" he asked, drawing her closer.

"No, I just need a drink. Want one?" Lacy pushed from his embrace, climbing from the bed. She reached for the black negligee, slipping it over her head, past her shoulders. Then with a little wiggle it slid over her hips. The transparent, silky material hung on every curve.

"Beautiful." Wyatt's head lay on his palm, propped up on one elbow. "Think I'll just lie here and drink in the scenery. You're gorgeous."

Lacy attempted a smile, but it caught in her throat.

"Is everything okay?" His brows creased as he began to rise from the bed. Sinewy muscles rippled over golden skin stretched taut across his chest. A powerful hand reached for her.

Dodging his grasp, she muttered, "Yeah, I just have a lot on my mind...things I have to do in the morning." Then she escaped through the door, leaving him and her dreams lying in her bed.

In the kitchen, Lacy opened the refrigerator door and paused, closing her eyes.

Why had she let this happen?

For years, she had done without sex, done without the emotional havoc of doomed relationships. Why hadn't she kept her zipper up and her legs crossed?

"Lacy?"

She startled, turning to find Wyatt's imposing body wedged in the kitchen's entryway. His large hands leisurely held onto the doorjamb. He had donned his jeans, but the button was undone, allowing a wisp of dark hair to peek out.

Carved muscle and steel. Lacy breathed in the sight.

She knew better than to want something she couldn't have. And Lacy wanted this man way more than was healthy.

Wyatt watched Lacy. He'd felt the ice in her touch when she pulled away from him in bed. Something had changed her mood and he had no idea what. Nothing he had said or done could've caused this mood swing.

"You okay?" he asked as he strolled her way.

"Yeah. Beer?"

Before he could answer, she ripped the six-pack open and grabbed a beer, popping the cap. The bottle hissed as she pushed the beer against his chest. Wincing against the chill, his fingers closed around the beer. Slowly, he brought the amber liquid to his lips and drank. The coolness felt good sliding down his parched throat.

Wyatt noticed that Lacy had yet to retrieve a drink for herself as she closed the refrigerator door. Had it been an excuse? Was she having second thoughts? How could she regret what had just happened?

There was something magical between them.

They fit together like a baseball in a catcher's mitt. Like a golf ball in the eighteenth hole. Briefly, he considered sharing his analogies with her, then hesitated. Most women didn't appreciate the analogies men made between them and sports.

For a moment, he was speechless. Then he asked, "Lacy, do you want me to leave?"

The thread of hope he'd held onto broke when she muttered, "It's probably for the best."

Aloof, she turned her back to him.

A flush of anger burned Wyatt's face. Evidently, this night didn't mean as much to her as it did him. He'd never chased a woman and he wouldn't start now. He sat his beer down on the table hard enough that he saw her startle at the *clunk*. Then he turned and headed for the bedroom.

After Wyatt dressed he entered the small living room, picked up his Stetson and beat it against his leg once before seating it firmly upon his head.

He took one more look around. Briefly, he thought of going to her, demanding she explain her change of heart. Instead, he said, "See you around, Lacy," and let the door swing shut with a bang.

Lacy cringed at the deafening sound of finality. She struggled not to run to the door, fling it open and beg him stay if only for the remainder of the night. A cold shiver shook her body from head to her toe. She closed her eyes as a heaviness descended upon her chest.

She had come alive in his arms. Remembered what she'd been missing. In this stranger's arms she had felt safe, cherished, even loved. She knew it was a whimsical fancy. Still, the tribulations of her life had vanished and for a moment she'd been at peace. Something she hadn't felt in a long time.

Why couldn't life be different, men be different? Braced against the kitchen countertop, Lacy felt her bravado shatter. Like a week-old cookie, she crumbled to her knees on the cold linoleum floor. Shaky palms covered her face as the dam broke and tears fell.

Chapter Four

ဆာ

Dreary. Dreary. Dreary. It was the only word Lacy could think of as she woke to thunder and the pitter-patter of raindrops beating against her bedroom window. Buried beneath the covers, she longed to smell the clean crisp air that the storm sounds promised. Yet she hated the thoughts of gray clouds and the sunless day ahead.

She pulled her arms out from under the comforter and began a leisurely stretch, when sudden pain stopped her short.

"Ow!"

An ache spread through her body, reminding her of the decadent night shared with her tall, dark cowboy. The pillow beside her still held the deep impression of his head. She rolled onto her side. Her fingertips lightly traced the indentation. She brought the pillow to her face. Eyes closed, she inhaled his essence. It was a heady blend of male, soap and sex. A wave of warmth built, shimmering across her body, tightening her nipples and heating the apex between her thighs.

A disgusted breath pushed from her mouth. How pitiful was she?

"Ughh..." Lacy grumbled and rose to a sitting position, then tossed the pillow across the room and watched it rebound off the wall. Tumbling onto her back, arms and legs spread-eagle, she stared at the chipped ceiling.

Last night had been a mistake. But what a heavenly mistake. She couldn't resist the smile that touched her lips.

She refused to be guilt-ridden. Things happened for a reason. The fact was, she'd needed a man. She'd needed the support his arms, his body—her grin widened—and his kisses had lent her.

This brief interlude was nothing compared to the other obstacles that life had thrown into her path. She'd be okay.

Things always looked better after a good night's sleep. If only Lacy had slept peacefully. A brighter picture, a better attitude—that was all she needed to get her through today.

There would be no regrets. Hell, she wouldn't even let the weather dampen her newfound encouragement.

Lacy threw back the covers and pushed from the bed. The alarm clock on the bedstand flashed eight o'clock in neon green. Four hours of sleep wouldn't help the final she had to take today.

Oh well, she was burning daylight. "First stop, the hospital. Second, school," she said as the bathroom door slammed shut behind her.

* * * * *

Every time Lacy stood before her daughter's hospital room, the blood in her head and ears roared, pounding like warring drums. Her hand trembled as she laid her palm against the cool metal door handle.

From one day to the next, she never knew what to expect. Would Jessie greet her with a kiss, or would she be too weak to even raise her head?

As Lacy pushed opened the door her heart stopped. A cluster of white-coated doctors surrounded her baby.

Had something happened?

Her muscles locked. Leaden feet refused to move. A wave of tears built, pushing against the back of her eyelids.

Then Dr. Lawrence turned and smiled. He raised his weathered hand in greeting. "Good morning, Ms. Mason. I hope you don't mind, but I've brought a couple of interns in to meet your beautiful daughter."

He stepped aside. Jessie came into view. The breath Lacy held rushed out in a single gust. Jessie's usually dull eyes sparkled with the attention that was being bestowed on her.

Lacy's heart melted with relief.

"Look, Mommy, I got a teddy bear." Jessie clung to the brown-tufted bear as if it were a prized possession.

"How wonderful. Did you thank the doctors?" Lacy asked as she approached.

"Uh-huh," her daughter's high-pitched, little girl voice chimed.

Lacy stilled, steadied herself. "How is she?"

"Good news," Doctor Lawrence said. "Jessie is fourth in line."

Good news... Good for whom?

The doctor's news could only mean one of three things. One, a recipient ahead of Jessie had perished; two, he or she had received a heart, which meant a donor had expired; or three, Jessie's condition had worsened.

The concern on Lacy's face must have been apparent. Dr. Lawrence quickly added, "A donor was provided for a patient ahead of Jessie. And your daughter is doing just fine."

He reached down and gathered Lacy's trembling hands in his. Gently, he squeezed. "Well, let's let mom and daughter visit, shall we?" he said, releasing her hands before ushering the students out the door.

"Mommy, did you bring me somepin'?" Jessie looked so small for a child of four. Her frail hand slowly caressed the bear she held to her chest.

"I did." Lacy swung her backpack onto the bed, unzipped one of the pockets, and extracted a handful of colorful ribbons—red, blue, green and yellow.

Wide-eyed, Jessie chirped, "Pretty!"

Lacy traced a finger down the upturned nose that mirrored her own. Jessie had more color in her cheeks this morning than she had yesterday.

Today was a good day.

"I thought if you were up to it, we'd braid these ribbons in your hair."

"Yeahhh," Jessie eagerly squealed as she attempted to pull herself up, unsuccessfully. Her golden eyes—so like Lacy's—saddened.

"Here, baby, let me help." Lacy used the controls to ease the head of the bed upward. Then she carefully arranged Jessie in a sitting position, shoving pillows around her for support.

From the backpack, Lacy retrieved a brush and comb. With care, she slipped the brush through her daughter's auburn curls.

Last night's rain had left the ground soft and wet. Gray clouds still moved steadily in from the West Coast. Another storm was coming.

Wyatt gazed down at his sodden boots, shook his head and closed his eyes. A night of pure heaven ended without the promise of another, followed by a fitful night's sleep and now this.

The roar of a truck barreling down the drive brought his head up and eyes open. Wyatt heard the slosh of mud splattering against his truck as Chance's red pickup passed and then came to a swaying halt.

Wyatt ran his fingers through his hair before settling his hat back on his head. He was in no mood for company. Yet he *had* offered Chance a place to stay while he was in town for the rodeo. In fact, his friend was always a welcome sight, just not today.

Dammit! The woman had Wyatt tied in knots. All he could do was think about her. But there were chores to do, animals to feed. Thank goodness he didn't have to go into the office today.

In the distance he heard Blue bark. His Queensland Heeler must have marked a rabbit. Just as the thought entered his mind a jackrabbit sprang from the sagebrush, Blue hot on its trail. The chase was on.

Did Lacy want him to chase her?

As Wyatt approached the corrals, he swore the horses standing in ankle-deep water glared at him. "Crap," he droned. "Forgot to open the stable doors. Sorry, boys."

The side door of the barn squeaked as he swung it wide and slipped inside to open the barn doors leading to the corrals. When he did, the horses rushed past him.

Ace whinnied, motioning his head toward the flakes of alfalfa hay Wyatt bent to retrieve. *Toss 'em, idiot*, the horse seemed to say, stomping his hooves impatiently. The other horses echoed Ace's sentiment.

Chance's truck door creaked, and then made a heavy thud as it slammed shut. Blue barked in welcome.

"Hey, old boy, caught a rabbit did ya?" Chance said. Wyatt heard his friend holler to him, "Didn't expect you home so early." When Chance entered the barn, he took one look at Wyatt and his cheery voice faltered. "You didn't just get home, did you?"

"No!" Wyatt's reply came out sharper than he had intended. Damn the woman. "But it appears you have." He scooped up a coffee can full of grain and poured it into Ace's feed bin. The bay quarter horse thrashed his head up and down in thanks.

Chance crouched, rubbing Blue's head. The dog's tail wagged with delight. "Ah, Wyatt, everyone has a dry spell." The man stood.

"Dry spell?" Wyatt's huff held irony. He had just experienced the best sex of his life with the woman of his dreams. And, the good ol' boy between his thighs wasn't going to let him forget it anytime soon.

His cock twitched, stirring to life as his pulse began to sing. Even now, the hot, carnal memories made him hungry for more. The need to press between Lacy's long legs had haunted him all morning long.

Not exactly what Wyatt would call a dry spell.

With a single finger Chance raised the rim of his hat. "Uh, does that grin mean the night wasn't a total bust?"

"Oh yeah, it wasn't all bad," Wyatt muttered, as he brushed his hands on his jeans. "Coffee's ready. Want some breakfast?"

As the men strolled silently back to the large Spanish-style house located in the southeastern part of Chandler, Chance raised a brow and asked, "Good?"

Wyatt looked past his friend glancing at the desert scenery. Greasewood, cactus and bright orange and blue Mexican bird of paradise sprang up around the house. A few queen palm trees broke up the natural terrain.

"No, not good. Amazing," Wyatt replied with the briefest of grins. He opened the back door of the house and stepped into the kitchen.

"Damn, I knew it." Chance shook his head and frowned, as if he suspected that the opportunity of a lifetime had passed him by. The screen door slammed behind him.

Within minutes Wyatt had bacon sizzling on the stovetop. Its greasy aroma filled the spacious kitchen. Decked out with every modern appliance, the kitchen was a cook's dream come true. Brass pots and pans hung over a large granite-topped island situated in the middle of the spacious kitchen.

For a moment Wyatt stopped and wondered what Lacy would think of his home. Would she enjoy sitting at the breakfast bar staring out the window and sharing each morning with him?

Now where had that impossible thought come from? He was a bachelor at heart. Even his mother and sister's constant nagging hadn't pushed him to the point of tying the knot.

Still, he couldn't stop thinking how she would look in his kitchen, his living room…his bed.

A knot formed in his stomach as he moved to the stove. He had to get the woman off his mind.

Wyatt scooped the last of the fried potatoes from the skillet into a bowl. A sudden pop turned his attention to the toaster as the bread shot up.

Hot. Hot. He juggled the warm bread in the air before tossing it on a plate.

Grabbing a piece of toast, Chance smeared it with butter then took an eager bite. He chewed as he mumbled, "Wyatt, where'd you learn to cook?"

"It was learn to cook or get married. I learned to cook." Wyatt added diced tomatoes, green chilies and cheese to scrambled eggs in a frying pan and stirred. The southwestern scent filled the air with a tantalizing aroma.

"How's the job?" Chance grabbed a piece of bacon and stuffed it into his mouth. "Heard you're a VIP or something."

"VP. Vice President." Wyatt shook his head. Chance knew exactly what VP stood for. His friend enjoyed playing the sorry-ma'am-I'm-just-a-cowboy role. He dressed the part, actually *lived* the part. But in reality, the man was a millionaire, an entrepreneur and a computer genius. Chance loved the rodeo. He didn't want to settle down, and he didn't have to.

"Never thought you'd leave the rodeo circuit." Another piece of bacon disappeared from the plate and into Chance's mouth.

Wyatt placed the eggs on the table. "Just left one circuit for another." He laughed at his own pun. Scooting out a chair, he sat down across from Chance.

Over the last five years, Wyatt had steadily moved up the ladder at the semiconductor firm he worked for in Tempe, Arizona. He'd done a damn good job of establishing himself. Still, he couldn't stop envying the man before him—and his freedom to follow the rodeo circuit.

In silence they ate, until Chance looked up from his plate. "Gonna see her again tonight?"

Wyatt blew the steam off the cup of coffee cradled in his palms. The rich scent of roasted beans wafted through the air. "Don't know."

Chance grinned, dishing another huge serving of potatoes onto his plate. "Never been a woman who could resist you, especially after she had a taste of you." His brows wagged.

Wyatt took a sip of his coffee. "This one's different."

"Don't tell me she used you for a one-nighter?" Chance chuckled at his own attempt at a joke. Wyatt's frown hushed him.

Inwardly Wyatt cringed, because that's exactly how he felt—used. Had it been a one-night stand to Lacy? Had she just wanted a taste of a cowboy?

Well, that's not what he wanted. And David Wyatt Anderson always got what he wanted.

His lips curled into a smile. Negotiations were about to begin.

Chapter Five

ᔕᑎ

"Lacy! Lacy!" The nurse nudged Lacy awake. "Honey, I think it's time for you to go. Don't want to be late for finals."

Lacy gazed up at the sweet, round face of Carol, the morning shift nurse.

Lacy had fallen asleep in the chair, her folded arms nestling her head as she leaned against Jessie's bed. Jessie, too, had slipped into slumber. But she looked more like an angel than the frumpy mess Lacy felt like.

Looking at her watch, Lacy sprang from the chair. "Thanks, Carol! I'll be back after school." She grabbed her backpack and headed for the door, then turned and dashed back to the bed, kissing Jessie softly on the forehead.

Adrenaline pumped through her veins as she fled from the hospital to her car. She just couldn't be late.

Parking was notoriously hard to come by at ASU, Arizona State University. Lacy's luck took a turn for the better as she spied a racy Corvette backing out. She pulled her clunky Ford Escort close, letting everyone know she had dibs on the parking spot. When the red sports car sped away, she spun her vehicle into the space.

Lacy briskly made her way to the two-story building that housed the Engineering Department. Swarms of people crowded the sidewalk as classes were dismissed and students fought their way to their next class.

Today was the last day Lacy would prowl the campus of ASU and it felt great. There was even a little bounce in her step that announced her excitement.

The auditorium reverberated with the sound of people filling it to its seams as Lacy entered. Backpacks dropped, feet shuffled, then all noise died away when Professor Tuttle approached the podium. The weasel-eyed man pushed his wire-rimmed spectacles up his stubby nose.

"Remove everything from your desk, except for Number 2 pencils, calculators and the test sheet."

He looked up at the clock, waiting, watching the minute hand inch closer to noon. When both clock hands met, he said, "Okay, you may begin."

Lacy inhaled a breath and a second wave of energy surged through her body. Shoulders squared, with confidence filling her, she knew she could ace the test in her sleep.

Forty-five minutes into the test, Lacy felt her strength and self-assurance falter.

Her mind went blank.

"No. Not now," Lacy said aloud. Her outburst received a scowl from Professor Tuttle and several students glared in her direction.

Breathe…focus, her mind directed. *You can do this in your sleep, remember?* the confident voice inside her reassured.

Lacy closed her eyes, inhaled and released a deep, calming breath. Yes, she could do this.

The next time Lacy looked up at the clock, it was 1:52. Eight minutes left, and she was finished. She sighed with relief.

She'd done it.

Chills skittered across her arms. After today, she would have a Bachelors of Science in Electrical Engineering in her back pocket, and a new job waiting for her Monday morning.

In anticipation of the new crop of engineering students graduating midterm, Dunbar Semiconductors had conducted campus interviews in November, just before Thanksgiving. Thankfully, she had nailed a position right here in the city.

No more drunks, rude comments and pawing hands at High Country. And no more forking out eight hundred dollars a month for Jessie's insurance. The child support she received—when she did receive it—only covered a fraction of the cost. The new job would provide steady hours and the opportunity for growth. The shabby apartment she'd been forced to take due to lack of funds would be in the past. If things worked out, Jessie would even have a bedroom of her own and Lacy a new car. The downside, of course, was that she would only have evenings and early mornings to spend with Jessie.

Life wouldn't change overnight, but Lacy could dream. Her degree and the new job were her first steps in the right direction.

After setting her test before the professor, she slipped out of the auditorium and headed toward her car. She climbed in, started the ignition and shifted into gear. As she pulled out of the parking space, she said, "Goodbye, ASU," and sped around the corner.

A newly found confidence blossomed inside Lacy as she maneuvered her car into the hospital parking lot. Bounding from the Escort, she couldn't wait to tell Jessie the news.

Hurried footsteps carried her down the hall, through the door and straight into her daughter's arms.

"I did it, Jessie. I did it." Lacy's cheeks ached from the tight smile on her face.

The little girl giggled and returned Lacy's hug. "Did what, Mommy?"

She hardly felt Jessie's tiny fingers around her neck. Jessie's strength was failing.

Lacy shook her head and pushed the depressing thought from her mind. Today was a day of celebration.

Lacy knew her child didn't understand the excitement she felt or why the slip of paper, a college degree, meant so much to her, to both of them.

Still, as Lacy unveiled the Cookies 'n' Cream ice cream she'd brought from Baskin-Robbins on her way to the hospital, Jessie knew they were celebrating something special.

At 6:00 p.m. Lacy watched an orderly set up a cot in the corner of the Jessie's room. He smiled. "Will you need more than one blanket, Ms. Mason?"

"No, Matt, one's enough."

The McDonald's charity, Ronald McDonald House, helped to provide housing for families with ailing children in residence at St. Joseph's Hospital. However, when Lacy stayed overnight, the staff graciously brought in a cot for her.

It was important to Lacy to spend as much time as possible with Jessie, especially on days like this, when her daughter was doing so well.

Most of their time spent together was quiet, tender moments. They gazed out the window at the lazy raindrops lightly falling, read, played games and shared stories of what had happened to each other during their time apart.

Last night's events flashed briefly in Lacy's mind. She felt the heat of her blush. That wasn't a story Lacy would share with her daughter. But it was a memory she would cherish. And on lonely nights when she needed comfort, she would think of her tall, dark cowboy.

Her body heated with the thought. She couldn't help but picture the sweet image of a man holding Jessie in one arm, his other wrapped around Lacy's shoulders.

Yearning was a terrible bedfellow. It left her feeling empty, lonely.

As Lacy's hand caressed Jessie's soft face, she wondered if she would ever find a man who could love her and Jessie. One who came home every night, who didn't chase the rodeo circuit. One she could trust. She thought of Wyatt and released a heavy sigh.

High Country was shaking at its seams. Cowboys were flooding into Arizona as if they rode the swells of a dust devil. Wyatt casually gazed around the bar as if looking for no one in particular.

Yeah, right. Chance didn't believe that one either. "Did you find her?"

"Who?" Wyatt replied nonchalantly, as he peeled the label from his Coors bottle and hoped he looked completely innocent.

"Who? C'mon, Wyatt, the person you dragged me down here to find. Lacy."

"Nah. And it was you who mentioned coming here tonight," Wyatt said as a blonde in tight fitting jeans snuggled up to him. The five-foot-six beauty bestowed a sexy smile upon him.

"Wanna dance, cowboy?" her sensual voice purred.

Wyatt plunked the bottle down on the bar. "Why not?"

As she led him upon the dance floor, the band began to play Garth Brooks' song "Rodeo". Their feet shuffled across the sawdust floor as Wyatt listened to the words of the song, reminding him why he'd quit the circuit.

The song's message that the rodeo controlled a man—so much so that he would give up everything, or anybody, just to play the game—touched too close to home. Too many of his friends had fallen into the clutches of rodeo fever. It was a madness that seeped into the blood, poisoning a man until he lived for nothing else.

Wyatt had seen his uncle go down that destructive path. At an early age Wyatt had sworn not to follow him. Still, he couldn't ignore the call to compete when it beckoned him, especially not when it was so close to home.

The body rub he was receiving from the sex kitten brought his attention back to her. His balls tightened, but not with the intensity that Lacy had induced. Just thinking of the woman he'd bedded last night made his cock harden and lengthen. He drew in a taut breath.

The woman deliberately brushed against his firm bulge and smiled. He returned the grin, knowing the gal would be pissed if she knew that he was thinking of another as he held her close.

"Wanna get out of here, cowboy?" The blonde ran a perfectly manicured fingernail up and down his arm. All he had to do was accept.

Instead he looked down at her. "No, thank you, ma'am."

You could've knocked them both over with a light breeze. She puffed up like a peacock, her feathers clearly ruffled as she jerked from his arms. Wyatt thought he heard her mutter "Asshole," as she spun around and stomped from the dance floor, leaving him alone among the many dancers bumping and grinding.

As he strolled through the crowd, he took off his hat and threaded his fingers through his black hair. What had gotten into him? He'd had a willing woman in his hands and let her slip away. Wyatt shook his head in disgust.

What man let a filly like that ride away? *A man with another woman on his mind.* Wyatt answered his own question as he reached for another beer.

When had he allowed Lacy to get under his skin? He grinned. It could've been any number of times he'd found himself buried deep inside her. Yet he knew the real answer. It was the way she'd felt in his arms, as if she belonged there.

Just then Chance sauntered up, grin on his face, a sexy redhead on his arm. "Wyatt, Rosy...Rosy, Wyatt." Chance's idea of introductions left much to be desired. "There's a party over at Rosy's house after the bar closes. Interested?"

The brassy redhead clung to Chance. Her body slid sensually against him. No secret on the outcome of the night for Chance.

"Nah, I ride tomorrow." Chance did too, but it was obvious that his friend wouldn't let this prime piece of flesh slip through his fingers.

"Whatever," Chance responded before he led the redhead onto the dance floor and into his arms.

Watching the couple spin made Wyatt dizzy. He'd had enough for tonight. He was going home. Maybe he'd swing by a certain woman's place on the way.

Lacy woke with a start, a cry on her lips. Her body ached, felt heavy and damp. Every inch of her skin glistened with a sheen of perspiration. She drew her sticky shirt from her breasts. It had been a dream, she realized as she attempted to ease her rapid heartbeat.

Yet it had felt so real. His touch, his kiss. Only a dream...but her body hummed with unfulfilled desire.

Dazed, she looked about the room, taking in her surroundings. No, this wasn't her bedroom, nor did a sexy, handsome cowboy lie beside her. Only silence and a slumbering child lay before Lacy. She watched the ragged rise and fall of Jessie's chest.

As Lacy brushed strands of damp hair from her face her arm grazed across a nipple, making her jump at its sensitivity. When she moved her leg and felt the heaviness between her thighs, she groaned.

Christ, she was a mess.

Had one night of reckless abandon driven her to this point? Evidently the answer was yes. Yet had she reached the point of no return? Could she go back to her lonely ways with a vow of celibacy only a nun should have to endure?

Her body screamed, *No, never!*, but her mind answered a definite, *Yes*.

That's just what she needed at 2:00 a.m., a war between body and mind. Wide awake, Lacy moved toward the window and peered out into the darkness.

The storm had passed, leaving puddles of water in the streets and drops of moisture like tears upon the trees. Pinpricks of light littered the black velvet sky. Brilliant, promising stars that her mother had told Lacy as a child, "Held little girls' hopes and dreams".

Which star held Jessie's wishes? Lacy's warm palm splayed against the cool glass, as if she sought to touch the brightest of them all.

Lacy's shoulders rose and fell. She released a deep, audible breath and tucked a strand of hair behind her ear.

Which star held *her* dreams?

Maybe she was asking too much from the Big Guy upstairs. Health for her daughter, a home filled with happiness, love and a man who came home each night.

Did such things even exist?

Chapter Six

ॐ

The ground rose up and met Wyatt as the steer slipped through his fingers and he landed with a hard thud. Pride bruised, his hip ached. To top it off, he peered through a cloud of dust into concerned eyes. Chance held Ace's reins as Wyatt stood and dusted off his backside.

Rainwater didn't stay long on the ground in this part of Arizona. The thirsty earth drank it down nearly as quickly as it fell. But there were still a few puddles here and there. One of which Wyatt had stepped in earlier. Caked mud still clung to his boots and pant legs.

Chance handed Wyatt his hat. "What happened?"

"Whadd'ya mean, what happened? I missed the damn animal's head," Wyatt snapped, jerking Ace's reins from his friend's hands.

Chance cocked a brow. "Hell, you never miss."

Wyatt threaded his gloved fingers through his hair. Beat his dusty hat several times against his leg, and then squared it on his head.

"I lost my concentration."

"Want another go?" Chance asked.

"Hell, yes, I want another go," barked Wyatt, sliding his boot into the stirrup and swinging his leg over the saddle. He competed in three hours. Evidently he needed more practice than he'd thought.

"Gordon, run another steer," Wyatt yelled to the cowboy sitting on the chute.

A brown Guernsey steer with white markings shot from the opening, the timing rope snapped, and Wyatt's and Chance's horses burst from the box, one on each side of the beast.

Chance was an excellent hazer, keeping the target within Wyatt's grasp as he leaned from the saddle. With ease, he dropped on the steer, grabbing its horns and bringing it down. The feeder mooed his annoyance as Wyatt raised him high in the air, and then twisted him to the ground. The animal's head and neck wrenched in Wyatt's iron grasp. The calf's chest heaved as he surrendered, lying docilely on his side.

Chance gathered up Ace's reins. "Yeah! That's how it's done."

Now, if only Wyatt could keep a certain woman off his mind long enough to compete, he'd have it made.

* * * * *

Two days had passed since Wyatt had last seen Lacy.

His hand slid over the steering wheel as he pulled his truck into High Country's parking lot. Without delay, he climbed out of the vehicle. As the door slammed his feet were already in motion. Just the thought of seeing her again played havoc with his hormones. Man, he wanted her.

"Hey, buddy." Wyatt looked over his shoulder to see Chance bringing up the rear. "Hell of a day." Chance shook Wyatt's extended hand. "Thought I might find you here."

Wyatt didn't respond, nor did he want to acknowledge the mischievous smile plastered on his friend's face.

Today had been a success. Both Chance and Wyatt qualified in their events. There was a festive atmosphere in the air as they entered High Country. It was only eight o'clock and already the place was bursting at the seams.

From the corner of his eye, Wyatt saw Lacy. She pushed through the crowd, hips swaying, as she made her way to a table full of loud cowboys. A smile tugged at his lips when she stabbed her pencil into the grabby hand that landed upon her hip. The cowboy drew back, shook his hand, then tipped his hat in apology as he laid a five upon her tray.

The cowboy had nerve. Still Wyatt couldn't blame the man. The sight of Lacy made him breathless. She was tempting, no, downright *decadent* decked out in a short, tight skirt that emphasized her long legs, a black silk camisole, its straps hanging off her bare shoulders, and shiny ebony boots. Just the right amount of cleavage showed. Hiding more than it exposed, it was enough to entice a man to work toward revealing the rest.

Threads of silvery laughter flowed from her full lips as she stopped and chatted with Larry at the bar. The man's deft hands moved quickly, filling her order as she waited.

As the band struck up another tune, the toe of her boot tapped along with the music. Her head swayed and her body gradually followed.

Her slow, sensual movements heated Wyatt's blood and his pulse began to race as he made his way toward her. Moving behind her, he drank in her scent. The woman's fresh, floral aroma was turning him upside down, inside out.

"Hey—" She startled and turned into him. Their eyes met and held in a fiery exchange. "Wyatt," she whispered.

"Lacy."

Nervously, she sucked in her bottom lip, ran her hand around the edge of the tray she held. She glanced down at the floor and broke the connection. "I need to deliver these drinks."

"Can we talk later?" Wyatt asked as his hand rose and stroked the softness of her camisole and the skin above the fallen strap.

"Talk?" Lacy glanced over his shoulder at a rambunctious bunch of cowboys calling to her. She made a gesture with her hand as if to say, *be there in a minute.* "Yes, okay. We can talk." She pushed past him, leaving him with that promise.

Wyatt saw both her reaction to him and her words as moving in a positive direction. Also, when he'd caressed her, his hand hadn't met the same fate as the previous man who had touched her.

A firm grasp clasped Wyatt's biceps. He turned to see Chance. "Got a table near the band. You gonna join us?"

Wyatt cocked one brow. "Us?"

"Rosy, the redhead." Chance's shit-eating grin grew as he led the way. "What can I say? She wants my body."

Us included Rosy's girlfriends, two big-breasted blondes. Sisters, they said, Jody and Joan. Wyatt felt as if he'd been thrown into a nest of black widows, each caressing his body with hungry eyes.

He shot Chance a heated glare. His friend returned it with a wink.

Damn the man. It appeared Chance was doing a little matchmaking of his own.

After Wyatt's second dance with each of the two blondes, he was determined to escape the trap closing in on him. Their strong, musky perfume was a noose tightening around his neck. When plans for the remainder of the night came up, he stood, excused himself and disappeared into the crowd.

Wyatt had plans of his own, and they included only one woman tonight.

A loud roar flooded the bar. Lacy was operating the bull.

When the cowboy hit the mat, Lacy wished it was Wyatt taking the fall. Regret filled her. She'd taken out her anger on the poor man she'd tossed from the bull. She needed to curb her temper.

So what if Wyatt was enjoying himself in the arms of other women? Still, it maddened her that he'd made plans to be with her tonight, but was off with not one, but two other women.

Well, he'd only said he wanted to talk.

She should've seen it coming. It was so typical...of a cowboy.

"Lacy, here's a twenty if you'll ride." Sam was up to his old tricks.

"No way," she responded with a chuckle.

Several other men freely offered up their money. Lacy hesitated. If only she'd worn jeans.

"You wouldn't dare." Wyatt's whiskey-smooth voice slipped down her spine. Her first reaction was desire. Her nipples tingled. Moisture built between her thighs. Then his words registered.

"What?" She gazed into the dusky blue eyes glaring at her.

"Look how you're dressed, Lacy. You're not riding, not tonight."

She glanced at her short skirt. Her brows knitted before she looked back to him and sputtered, "As if you have any say." Her attempt to rise was stopped short by a strong hand pushing down on her shoulder.

"You're not riding." It was a demand—not a request, not a suggestion. Sparks ignited in his eyes as he pinned her with a glare that sent chills down her back.

There was something exciting about his domination. Still, Lacy was an independent woman.

"Back off, Wyatt. I'll ride if I want to." Lacy rose, avoiding his grasp.

God, what was she thinking? She'd had no intentions of riding. Yet she wouldn't allow a man to dictate what she would or wouldn't do. Especially one she'd only met for the second time tonight.

Lacy's heart fluttered as he stormed after her like a jealous boyfriend. Her only thought was to flee, but she wasn't quick enough. She gasped as his fingers folded around her arm like a vise.

"Lacy, your boyfriend's right. You're not riding," barked Larry. His pudgy fists were buried deep into his hips. The crowd had begun to rumble with excitement. Larry must've sensed the danger, as he stood flanked by two bouncers. "Get your ass back in that chair."

How humiliating. Heat flooded her face. She jerked her arm, but she was unable to shake Wyatt's iron grip.

She hadn't had a man tell her what to do in ages. And, she wouldn't start now.

"How dare—" Her words were silenced as Wyatt's lips found hers. Firmly, he took her into his arms. It was an arrogant, masculine show of ownership. Lacy hated how it made her feel—like she couldn't get enough. Her traitorous body melted in his embrace, giving as much as it received, responding to his touch, his taste.

"Okay, big boy, you've staked your claim. Now let her get back to work," grumbled Larry, unable to hide the grin behind his words.

Talk about embarrassing. First, she made a total ass out of herself by threatening to ride the damn bull, in a skirt no less. She'd have been airing her pussy for all to see. Second, she'd given the crowd a show. And third, her boss had all but given her away to Wyatt.

The masculine camaraderie Wyatt sent Larry in the way of a wink was the icing on the cake.

"Argh!" she groaned, jerking from Wyatt's arms and storming out of the bar.

Cool, crisp air greeted her like a slap to the face. It stung, or was it the heat of anger that burned her cheeks?

"Lacy." Wyatt's heavy footsteps pounded behind her.

She held up a single hand, silencing him as she began to aimlessly pace the parking lot. She had to work off some of the fury that raged inside.

"I—"

She halted. Glared up at him. Her mouth opened then snapped shut before she continued past the cars and trucks into a small opening.

Finally, she turned to confront the man steps away from her. "I have never—" Her words faltered.

She couldn't continue, not with him looking at her the way he was.

The light from a streetlamp lit his face as he stepped from the shadows. Desire flared in his eyes, a raw hunger that called to its mate. Like a match to kindling, her body went up in flames. Her breasts grew heavy, taut with need.

Without another word she found herself pressed against his muscular chest, strong arms holding her with such tenderness she felt it straight to her heart.

Had he come to her or did she go to him? All senses left her when Wyatt was around.

"Stop, Wyatt," she moaned as he rained a trail of soft kisses across the top of her breasts, exposed by the camisole he was slowly pulling down.

Through the silky material he caught a nipple between his teeth and tugged. A quiver shook her body.

"Wyatt," she whimpered again, wanting, needing for him to strip her naked and take her right here, right now. Liquid heat pooled between her thighs.

"Let me make love to you tonight." His voice was pure seduction as his hand slipped beneath her shirt and bra and began to caress a sensitive breast. "I promise you'll enjoy the things I'll do you to."

Lacy knew he would live up to his wicked promise. She answered him by inching her hand down and inside the front of his pants. The hiss of his breath as her fingers curled around his cock was exciting, arousing. He was hard in her hand. The apex between her legs began to pulse with anticipation as she fondled and felt him grow firmer.

"Whoa!" Wyatt grasped her hand and stilled it. His breath came in a short, quick cadence. Carefully, he withdrew her hand from his jeans. "I have a better place in mind. Besides, Larry said to have you back in five minutes."

"Damn him. Damn you," she spat, balling her fists.

He stroked her as if she was a kitten. "Now, honey, you don't mean that."

"Yes, I do," she insisted, loving the feel of his hands over her heated skin. She wanted him inside her, stroking her pussy. Her desire dampened her panties and made her breasts ache to the point of discomfort.

Strong arms embraced her, drawing her within the security of his arms. "No, you don't," he whispered as his teeth nibbled on an earlobe.

"Okay, okay. No, I don't," she admitted, leaning into him. "Still, I've got to get going. If I'm not back soon, Mark will come looking for me. He acts like my own private bodyguard."

"All right, but no riding the bull." A brow rose as if seeking her agreement, but she knew it was a command. And right now this man could command her anytime.

"No, riding the bull...until later tonight." Her palms playfully skimmed down his chest feeling the pebbling of his nipples as she brushed past them. "Then I'm going to ride him hard and put him up wet."

"Christ, Lacy, what you do to me," he groaned, releasing her.

"Until tonight." She threw the wicked promise over her shoulder as she turned.

"Yeah, but it better go quickly," Wyatt said as he hurried to catch up with her. Hand in hand, they made it back into the bar.

The night crawled at a snail's pace. Lacy was everywhere but where he wanted her. In his arms, beneath him.

Brushing a hand through his hair, he sighed. Wyatt had never wanted a woman the way he wanted Lacy. He ached to touch and be touched by her. He needed to be buried deep inside her, to revel in her moans of passion as she climaxed in his arms.

His emotions were confusing and a little frightening.

"Wyatt, Rosy—"

"Got plans, Chance," Wyatt interrupted, nodding toward Lacy just as a man came up behind her and grasped her by the waist. Raising her into the air, he spun her around.

Wyatt heard her squeal of surprise, then saw all color drain from her face when she turned and saw who embraced her.

Slowly, Wyatt stood.

Playfully the man led her out onto the dance floor. Lacy resisted, but he held her tight.

Already once tonight Wyatt had played the jealous boyfriend. She'd probably kick his ass if he tried again.

He looked for the large bouncer who always seemed to be around when Lacy needed him.

Strange. Mark stood at the sidelines and watched as if he was helpless to interfere.

Foreboding seeped inside Wyatt as he moved in the direction of the couple. A firm hand to his chest brought him to a sudden halt.

"You don't want to mess with that one," Chance warned. His friend's seriousness was apparent in his tense jaw and narrowed eyes. "That's Mad Dog Mason."

"Is that supposed to mean something to me?" Wyatt asked, his palms itching to remove the man's arms from around Lacy's waist.

"Mad Dog Mason almost killed a man for messing with his rigging. Ah, shit..." Chance groaned, his eyes drifting shut as he shook his head.

"What?"

Chance's Adam's apple slid up and down as he swallowed. "I thought I'd seen Lacy before, but I didn't make the connection."

Wyatt was sure he didn't want to hear any more, but he still asked, "Seen her before?"

"You've been away from the circuit off and on." Chance's hand jutted out, halting a passing waitress. He gazed down at her nametag. "Helen, what's Lacy's last name?" he asked.

Suspicious, she glared at him. "Why?"

"I'm just curious." Chance shrugged as if it didn't make a difference to him whether she told him or not.

"Mason, Lacy Mason."

"Thanks, darlin'." Chance graced her with a smile and placed a five on her tray. When she was out of earshot, Chance removed his hat, ran a wary hand across his forehead, and muttered, "Shit, man! He's crazy. You don't want to mess with him." Chance shook his head. "But it's too late. You've fucked his wife."

Chapter Seven

℘

Chance's words hit Wyatt with the force of a five-hundred-pound boulder to the chest. He flinched. "Wife?"

"I'm sorry, Wyatt. I didn't realize..."

Chance's apology was dismissed with a wave of Wyatt's hand. Slowly, he sank into his chair, placing his folded arms on the back of the chair in front of him. "She never told me she was married." He looked at the couple dancing as one.

Lacy moved instinctively, as if she knew the man's—her *husband's*—next move. Then she stopped, gracing Mad Dog with a smile that made Wyatt's stomach clench.

"They never do," Chance replied matter-of-factly, frowning at the woman. "C'mon, buddy, let's get out of here." He made a gesture that seemed to say, *right now, before it's too late.*

But it was already too late.

The betrayal and pain that Wyatt felt began to slowly, dangerously, manifest into anger, a heated emotion that brought him to his feet. Flames of red-hot fury licked up his neck, scorching his face and ears.

He had acted the fool over this woman.

"Wyatt?" Chance's fingers closed over Wyatt's biceps. "Hey, Wyatt?"

"Yeah?" Wyatt's baritone tone was eerily calm.

"I don't like the look in your eyes." Chance pulled at him. "C'mon, let's get out of here."

Wyatt glared down at Chance's hand. The expression he threw Chance must have hit its mark as the man's hand dropped and he took a step backward.

"Okay, okay…" Chance looked around the room. "I'll gather the boys."

Wyatt chuckled softly. Chance was expecting trouble, big trouble. "No need. I'm just gonna have a little talk with the lady, a talk that we should've had Wednesday night when we first met." *Before I fell for her and let her lead me around by my cock.*

Dazed, Lacy looked at the man who seductively grinned at her. At one time she'd flipped over the sexy cowboy, but no longer. Her ex-husband wore his cowboy hat low to hide his horns. He was the devil incarnate.

When he swung her into his embrace, his breath swept across her heated neck. He smelled of aftershave, beer and tobacco as he firmly pressed their bodies together.

It was fascinating how they moved together as one. Dancing was one of the things Lacy missed after their breakup. And Jay was sinfully good at it.

"I've missed you, doll," he whispered softly in her ear, lightly nibbling on her earlobe.

"Don't!" Lacy tensed and missed a step.

"Ah, darlin', don't be that way," he groaned, his body moving against hers as if making love to her.

Breathlessly, she demanded, "Jay, let me go. There's no way —"

"…that you'll let me make love to you," he chuckled. "Your mouth says no, but your body is saying yes." The palm resting in the small of her back tightened and pressed their hips closer. She felt his erection nudge the apex of her thighs.

"You're wrong, Jay. I don't want you." Lacy's feet froze, drawing both of them to a sudden stop. A couple moving across the floor bumped into them and then continued dancing as if they were a minor disturbance.

Lacy smiled. She *didn't* want Jay. The knowledge was an awakening. It was over, truly over.

Wyatt, her conscious spoke his name and her body tingled, warming, as her gaze sought him. She couldn't wait to be in his arms.

Their eyes met, locked. He watched her with an expression she didn't quite comprehend. Was he mad, jealous? The thought raised the hairs on her arms. He had given her so much, including the confidence and strength to say goodbye to the past, to Jay.

"Ah, doll, I thought we got past all that stuff. What about Jessie?"

Lacy's head snapped up. Her eyes burned as she glared at Jay. How dare he mention their daughter's name now, when he hadn't even asked about her to begin with?

"It's over, Jay. It's been over for a long time." She slipped from his arms. "Do you even know how Jessie's doing? Of course you don't. You don't see her, you don't ask about her, you don't do a damn thing for her." She turned, leaving him speechless and alone in the middle of the dance floor.

God, that felt good. Lacy's arms hugged her midriff. She'd done it. She'd walked away from Jay without an ounce of regret, without unsatisfied desire simmering in her belly. She was finally free.

Lacy felt the heat of Wyatt's body before she saw him standing in the shadows against the wall. She went to him and eased her arm around his neck, tugging him down until their mouths met. The soft, gentle kiss she had intended morphed into a meshing of teeth and tongue, a violent assault that stole her breath. She trembled, moved her palms between them and shoved.

Strong hands clasped her wrists, and then drew them above her head, as Wyatt whipped her around and his body drove hers against the wall.

Lacy's breathing was labored as she fought the swelling panic. She raised her knee between his thighs in warning and nudged. Abruptly, the kiss ended.

"What the hell is wrong with you?" Lacy snapped, fighting to gain composure. She swallowed hard and attempted to jerk her bound hands out of his, unsuccessfully. "Let me go," she growled.

Then she stilled, gazing into the depths of his eyes. They burned with a red-hot fury.

"When were you going to tell me?" he demanded. The pressure on her wrists increased. His hold bit into her tender skin.

"Tell you what? Wyatt, you're scaring me." Nervously, Lacy looked around for Mark. Where was the man when she needed him?

"That you're married," his voice was harsh, condemning.

"Married! Is that what this is about?" An agitated laugh pushed through her clenched teeth. "You idiot. I'm divorced. And, it wasn't…isn't any of your business."

The grip on her wrists relaxed and he released her. She brought her hands in front of her and looked at the angry marks he'd left. She looked up at him, shook her head and turned to leave.

"Lacy, wait."

"You've got to be kidding me." She glared at him. "Wait? Wait for what? Wait for you to hit me?" Her stubborn chin rose. "Take your best shot, buddy. It'll be your last."

Lacy turned to move, but Wyatt was quick to block her departure. "Just give me a minute to explain." He hesitated, until she began to move, again. "It's just," he brushed a palm across his forehead. "It's just," he repeated. "Dammit, woman, you drive me crazy. When I saw you dancing…heard the man was your husband—"

"Ex-husband," she corrected.

"Well, that's not the way I heard it."

"Then before assaulting me, maybe you should've asked." After a moment of thought, she exploded in anger. "What kind of woman do you think I am?" She rose on her tiptoes, met him eye to eye. "You arrogant bastard. I've slept with two men in my life. Him…" She looked at Jay. As she'd anticipated, he had already chosen another bed partner for the night. He held a little blonde in his arms, his mouth near her ear. The smooth-talking devil was reeling the woman in by the looks of her dreamy eyes.

"…and you." Her gaze met Wyatt's again. "God, I was such a fool falling into bed with another cowboy." Disgust and regret rang in each of her words. Her eyes closed. She rubbed her palms briskly over her face. Man, she was tired.

"Lacy, I'm sorry—"

"Sorry?" she interrupted, opening her eyes wide. Had a man *ever* apologized to her? Not that she could remember. Jay never had.

"Yeah. I made an ass of myself." Wyatt's hesitant touch on her shoulder sent a wave of heat across her body. She saw the sincerity in his eyes, sensed it in his soft caress. "Can we put it behind us?"

Desire slammed hard, low in her belly.

She was a fool.

Lacy wanted this man, even if it was only for an hour, a night, a day or a weekend. He could be hers and she could make love to him until the rodeo ended and the call of another show lured him to the next town. She knew that letting him go would rip the heart from her chest. Yet doing without him was killing her. Her breasts ached, needing to feel his touch.

"Yes," Lacy murmured as her cell phone screeched. She drew it out of her skirt pocket and looked at the screen. "Oh God."

It was the hospital.

The warm blood flowing through Lacy's veins froze. She struggled to respond to the words droning in her ears.

"Jessie's blood pressure is dropping," said the nurse on the other end of the telephone. "Perhaps you should come to the hospital." A pause. "Ms. Mason, are you there? Hello?"

Lacy responded with a silent, weak nod of her head.

"Ms. Mason, hello?"

"Y-yes, I'm here," Lacy's voice cracked. "I'll be there in thirty minutes." The telephone snapped shut. She whirled away from Wyatt as her shoulders started to shake. Then she darted for the bar. "Larry…Larry, I have to go."

Wyatt followed close at her heels. "Lacy, what's wrong?"

"Is it Jessie?" The concern in Larry's voice was obvious as he reached beneath the counter and retrieved her purse. She grabbed it.

Her head moved in quick, short nods. Her voice was trapped in her tightening throat. The noises in the bar seemed to fade. She barely heard Larry speaking to her. Wyatt said something that she couldn't comprehend. Panic slid across her skin.

She had to get to Jessie.
Now!

Chapter Eight

ဆ

Jessie? Who the hell was Jessie? Wyatt looked at Lacy and then back at her boss.

"Do you need someone to drive you?" Larry offered, moving from behind the bar to take her in his arms.

Lacy shook her head, tears filling her eyes.

"Call me," Larry muttered in her ear and then released her.

Again, the quick, short nod.

What was going on? The telephone call had drained the color from Lacy's face. She was white as a sheet. Her eyes were moist. She trembled as if caught naked in a snowstorm.

In the crush of people she pushed, shoved and cleared a path as she made her way to the exit and burst through the door. The minute she made it outside, she broke into a run, heading to her car.

"Lacy!" Wyatt yelled as he followed and caught up with her. Slowly, she turned to face him. The haunted, painful expression in her eyes was gut-wrenching.

"Lacy, what's wrong?" Gently his hand brushed the hair from her face.

"My daughter." She knotted her fists into his shirt. Deep, dark desperation lay in the depths of her golden eyes. "My d-daughter needs a heart...blood pressure dropping..."

Lacy collapsed as if her legs refused to hold her. Wyatt heard his shirt rip as she slipped. Just in time, he caught her and pulled her trembling body against his chest. She shook, her teeth rattling. Then as if the sky had opened up, she started to cry.

"What hospital?" Wrenching sobs drowned out his words. "Lacy, what hospital?" he asked, again, shaking her softly.

"St. Joseph's," she said between hiccups. Her face buried into his shoulder, her tears soaking his shirt.

"C'mon, baby, let's go." The death grip around his neck remained as he lifted her into his arms and headed toward his truck.

Cars and stoplights were a blur as he raced across town to get Lacy to her daughter. He glanced down at the woman as she gazed blindly out the window. She was dry-eyed now. Still, her anguish was undeniable.

What must she be going through?

Where was her daughter's worthless father at a time like this? Shit. He knew the answer. Mad Dog Mason was in the arms of another woman.

Wyatt silently swore. He'd kill the sonofabitch next time he saw him.

When the truck came to a stop in the hospital parking lot, Lacy threw the door open and bolted for the hospital entrance. Wyatt followed her past the glass doors, down one corridor and then another, until she came to a sudden halt outside of room 1105.

She laid her palms upon the door, but she didn't move, made no attempt to enter. A sharp pain pierced his heart as she gazed up at him, an expression of raw fear reaching out to him.

A silent prayer left his lips as he wrapped his arm around Lacy's shoulders, grabbed her hand with his free one, and pushed open the door with his hip.

Wyatt felt Lacy's grip tighten. A single nurse stood over the small form curled atop a bed. He'd never seen so many machines, wires and tubes sprouting from someone so young. A subdued beep radiated from one machine. Others flashed lights, graphs and numbers. The scene before him was enough to bring a strong man to his knees.

How did Lacy face this each day?

The redheaded nurse turned and smiled. Lacy's mouth opened, but the woman silenced her, placing an index finger against her own rosy lips. Quietly, she motioned them to follow her.

In the hall, the woman began, "Mr. and Mrs. Mason. I'm Nancy. I'll be filling in for Jessie's regular nurse tonight—she's out sick." Lacy didn't correct her assumption, neither did Wyatt.

"I'm sorry to put you through such a scare. Jessie had a reaction to one of the medications. After I called you, her blood pressure rose and her vitals returned to normal. She's weak, but the doctor thinks she'll be just fine." The nurse squeezed Lacy's forearm. "The doctor will be in tomorrow to speak to you."

All bone mass seem to dissolve in Lacy's body, as she melted against Wyatt. He held her tightly, rejecting the urge to cradle her in his arms like a child. For now, he would be her support, her rock.

The nurse smiled again. "Take your wife in to see your daughter. She needs to see for herself Jessie's okay."

Wife? Daughter? It was a simple mistake anyone could make. Goose bumps slid across his skin.

Wyatt led Lacy further into the room. The child slept quietly. Her face was ashen, but there was a spot of pink on each cheek. Auburn lashes edged the hollowness of each eye. She had an itty-bitty nose that tipped upward just like her mother's. The girl sparked a tenderness in him that Wyatt never knew existed.

In quiet awe, he watched Lacy. As if she took inventory, she touched each finger, ran her hands up the girl's arms, caressed her face, then leaned over and kissed her. Lacy didn't stop there as she drew down the blankets, examined each leg and gently ran her hands over Jessie's feet. Then she pulled the blankets back over her daughter and tucked them tightly around her. Again, she kissed the girl's forehead.

Next, she turned her attention to the machines and monitors, studying them. When she appeared satisfied, her shoulders rose and fell as she released a heavy sigh.

Lacy turned and looked at Wyatt. He had been supportive, wonderful in the crisis. With no hesitation, he'd held her, lent her his strength. She wouldn't have made it through the night without him. She felt on the precipice of something she couldn't name.

Strong arms embraced her, as if he sensed her need. "Thank you," she murmured into his chest, breathing in his scent of spices and masculinity.

His response was a light kiss on her forehead as he sat down in the overstuffed green chair next to the bed, pulling her onto his lap. Cradled in his arms, she snuggled closer and listened to the soft beat of his heart. So like him— strong, steady. If only Jessie's heart beat the same way.

"Let me take you home. You need rest," he said, showering little kisses across her cheek, down her neck.

"I can't leave." Lacy's eyes drifted closed, enjoying his tender, comforting touch.

With the sound of a throat being cleared, Lacy's eyes shot open. The redhead nurse smiled. "Ummm...sorry to interrupt."

Lacy pushed from Wyatt's lap, feeling the same shade of pink on the nurse's face flood across her own.

"I just spoke with Dr. Lawrence. He said I should assure you that Jessie is out of danger. Her vital signs are stable. He also said for you to go home. He'll see you at ten o'clock tomorrow."

Wyatt rose to stand beside her.

Lacy shook her head. "No. I can't leave her."

"Dr. Lawrence said if you refused, I should throw you out." The sheepish grin on the nurse's face told Lacy she wouldn't dare.

Wyatt's arm snaked around Lacy's shoulders, drawing her nearer. "Doctor's orders, Lacy," he said. Then the rogue winked at the nurse, causing another blush to fan the woman's face.

"Mrs. Mason, you're a lucky woman," the nurse chuckled. "An angel for a daughter and a devil for a husband." Lacy didn't know the new nurse, but she liked her. Still she felt it necessary to correct the woman's assumption regarding Wyatt.

"No, he's not—"

"Come on, Wife, let's go home," Wyatt interrupted. A wicked grin flashed across his face. His words startled Lacy, leaving her speechless and she let him lead her out of the room.

Wyatt's heavy footsteps followed Lacy into the darkened apartment. Without a word, he brushed past her and headed for the bathroom. When she heard the water pipes whine and the flow of water splattering the bottom of the bathtub, she wondered what he was up to.

"Strip." Startled at the command, Lacy spun and stared at the imposing man standing in the doorway of her bedroom. The breadth of his shoulders almost encompassed the entire space.

As if jet-propelled, her heart took off. The pounding of her blood as it swirled through her body rang loud in her ears.

Lacy didn't know if it was the scare of Jessie's situation, but she needed Wyatt in some primal way. Needed his comfort, his embrace, needed to touch him, to feel him, to have something solid in her life at this moment. She needed him inside and out.

Tomorrow morning she would hear the doctor say Jessie would be all right. Jessie had to be, because Lacy would accept nothing less.

Until then…

"I ran a bath." He jerked his thumb toward the bedroom. "While you bathe, I'll get you something to eat. Is Wendy's okay? A hamburger? Or would you prefer a cheeseburger?"

"I'm not hungry."

"You have to eat some—"

She moved into his arms and gently pressed her lips against his. "What I need, what I'm hungry for…is you."

She stepped away from him, pulled the black camisole over her head and slung it across the room. She felt a sudden sense of freedom, as if some of the weight was being lifted from her shoulders. She needed this. Needed him.

The black strapless bra was gone with a quick twist of her fingers. She heard him groan. His eyes fixed on her breasts.

Okay, this was good. He was interested.

"Lacy, you need rest." His mouth moved, but his eyes remained locked on her naked breasts.

"What I need...is you." With a little wiggle of her hips, the skirt slid down her legs, pooling at her ankles before she stepped out of it. Wyatt's eyes widened as she hooked her thumbs into the elastic of the ebony lace panties and disposed of them quickly.

Clad now in only her boots, Lacy flashed him a come-and-get-me look. "Ride me, cowboy?"

Wyatt audibly choked. His features twisted into an expression of anguish. "Not tonight, Lacy. You've been through too much. Rest...you need rest," he insisted, the huskiness of his voice not at all convincing.

"No?" A finger disappeared between her pouty lips. The wet digit reappeared and then slowly traced a path around a taut nipple. Her eyes closed and her head lolled back.

She gasped as her areola puckered.

"You're killing me," he moaned. She heard his boot thump against the floor as he took a step toward her.

"Ummm..." Her eyes opened, she looked up through feathered lashes as her finger left her breast and brushed down her ribcage to her abdomen. "No?" She paused.

Did she dare?

What the hell. She pushed her finger into the nest of brown curls at the apex of thighs. Swollen to the touch, she felt the wetness, her heat, as a shiver exploded through her body. Her clit was bulging, aching to be caressed. Obligingly, her finger slid over it, creating more tremors.

Then she held the damp finger, drenched in her essence, for Wyatt to view. She felt naughty, sinful, as she whispered, "Do you want a taste, cowboy?"

As she watched the man's will crumble before her, Lacy felt like a demolitions expert igniting a fuse of dynamite under a tall building.

"God, Lacy, I don't know whether to groan, growl or grovel." In the end, Wyatt released a growl, then like a predator, strong and sleek, he strode toward her.

White-hot lust sparked in his eyes, sending a wave of excitement coursing through Lacy. Powerful hands scooped her into his arms and headed for the bedroom.

"You're a damn tease, little lady," he ground out through clenched teeth as he set her on her feet.

Lacy laughed. It felt good to laugh, especially after the hellish night she'd had.

She gasped at the sight of the sculpted ridges of Wyatt's abdomen as his shirt fell to the floor. He made several hops as he pulled off his boots and quickly stepped out of his pants.

She watched his cock thicken between his brawny thighs, tilting upward as it grew longer, harder.

Yes, Lacy would enjoy this tall, dark cowboy one more time.

When Wyatt was within arms length of Lacy, she wrapped her arms around his neck and pulled him to her. He surrendered without a struggle. If this was what she needed, he would oblige.

In a whirlwind of emotions, their mouths met. Wyatt swore he tasted heaven between her soft, willing lips as he plunged deeper into their silky depths. She responded by sucking on his tongue, nipping his bottom lip, before lolling her head back, giving him access to her neck.

Grabbing her by the waist, he raised her and she locked her legs around his back. Warm boots rubbed his back as he strolled to the bed. His erection nudged her pussy and he felt her welcome wetness on his cock as he gently lowered her body.

"As sexy as you look in those boots," he said, "they're going to have to go."

Lacy giggled as he laid her on the soft comforter. She propped herself up on her elbows. "Turn around, cowboy." When he did, she slipped a foot between his parted thighs. He felt the heel of her other boot press into an ass cheek and his cock stiffened. "Pull," she purred. Her boot and sock slid free and hit the floor with a thump when he tossed it aside. She used her naked foot to caress his erection, smoothing over his taut balls before she withdrew and placed her other boot between his legs. He pulled, and then pivoted.

Blood rushed to his groin. This woman was a delightful surprise he wanted to learn more about. Remembering the bathwater, he dashed into the bathroom, turned off the faucet and returned. He quickly donned a condom and then crawled beside her on the bed.

As she moved into his arms, he felt good knowing that, other than her ex-husband, no man had ever touched her. Lacy was naturally sensual as she slid her body against his, inviting him to caress, to taste.

When his mouth latched onto a taut nipple, a moan pushed from her full lips. He nipped and tugged and sucked until she arched into him. Then he released her and laved her other breast.

"Wyatt, I need to feel you inside me." Her hands tightened on his biceps. Her body tensed beneath his touch.

"You'll have to wait, baby. I'm not through tasting you."

Lacy groaned, her hips writhing beneath him, lifting off the bed to get closer to his cock.

"Be good or I'll stop."

"You wouldn't dare."

Licking a path from between her succulent breasts to her bellybutton, he felt the tremor that shook her.

"Wyatt?" Her hips rose as if seeking his mouth.

"Soon, baby." He spread her legs, kissing the soft skin inside her thighs. Her desire rose, sweetening the air. He inhaled, breathing in her essence before his tongue laved her pussy.

His touch surprised her and sent her hips bucking off the bed when he thrust his tongue deep inside her.

"Ahhh…"

From between her thighs he could see the rapid rise and fall of her chest. Her eyes were closed. Her jaw was clenched. The aroused expression on her face made his cock jerk, increasing his need to bury himself deep into her hot, wet pussy.

Instead, he nuzzled her folds before tracing them with his tongue until he found her swollen clit. As his lips latched onto the bud, Lacy's hands threaded through his hair, holding his face to her sex. Her hips rose, and she ground against him as his tongue pierced her core.

"Oh, Wyatt." She squirmed as he dipped deeper. She was sweet to the taste, soft to the touch as he stroked and caressed her body.

"Wyatt!" She opened her legs wider, pressing her heat firmly against him. Then her body tensed, convulsed as her pussy spasmed, jerking her entire body in one wave after another. She screamed in wild abandon, bucking against his face.

When the last tremor subsided, the most blissful expression softened her face. She exhaled, releasing her breath with a sigh. Then her eyes fluttered open. She smiled and opened her arms to receive him.

God, the woman took his breath away.

Lacy's skin was warm, damp with perspiration as he crawled atop her. She was even hotter and wetter between her thighs as he nudged his cock into her pussy. Each inch of penetration elicited a whimper of pleasure from her mouth, encouraging him to fill her. And he did.

With each slow thrust her hips rose to meet his. She locked her legs around him, pulling him closer, deeper.

Their mouths melded in a kiss of exquisite passion. He caressed her lips and delved between them. Did she like the taste of herself upon his tongue? The thought heated his blood, increasing the rhythm of his strokes.

The sound of flesh slapping flesh filled the air.

Chills raced up his spine as her fingernails glided lightly from his ass to the small of his back and across his shoulder blades.

When her claws bit into his skin, he knew she was close to another climax.

"Come, baby," he whispered in her ear, setting her off like a stick of dynamite. Her body arched off the bed. A groan wrenched from her throat.

She was so responsive.

Wyatt felt the ripples of her contractions squeeze his cock, and he was a goner. Blood roared in his head as he strained, the pull of his orgasm against his balls and cock making his breath catch in his throat.

She held him tight, taking all he had to give as his hips ground into hers.

The soft mewling sounds she made drove him crazy. The tender emotion on her face was breathtaking. She made him feel as if he were the only man in the world.

She grunted as his weight pressed her deep into the mattress, but she smiled and didn't complain. Carefully, he rolled over and took her with him so she lay atop him.

His gaze met hers as he held her close to his heart.

Wyatt had fucked his share of women, but no one had touched his soul like this one.

Something inside Lacy had fractured, snapped. She felt raw and exposed. But, Lord, she felt good lying on Wyatt. He was so big and warm and hard. His body fit hers perfectly.

A sense of rightness settled over her as she lay in his arms, her heartbeat finally returning to normal. It was right to be here with him. Because—

Because she'd fallen for him.

Her breath caught in her throat as she realized the truth. She had irrevocably—and inconceivably—fallen for a man she hardly knew. And a cowboy at that.

She tensed.

Wyatt buried his nose in her hair. She heard his deep intake of air, before he hugged her tighter. The thick ridge of his erection pressed between her thighs.

"Baby, whatever it is, don't bring it to bed." He slid her off his chest, spooning her back against his length. Then he began to stroke her, making small soothing circles around her breasts, cupping them and thumbing their peaks. "For tonight, let's pretend everything is okay," he whispered in her ear. "Let me love you," he said as his hips moved, easing his cock back and forth against her sex.

Lacy withdrew, turning to face him. A random tear raced down her cheek, disappearing among the sheets. "Hold me, Wyatt," her throaty voice begged. "Just hold me."

And without hesitation, he did.

A stream of light burst through the parted curtains, blinding Wyatt as he woke to the rustling of Lacy moving about the room. A pair of blue jeans slid up her long legs and a little wiggle brought them over her hips.

Lord, she had a great ass. He rose, elbow bent, his cheek resting on his fist as he took in the sight. She moved quietly, gracefully in the dusky room as she picked up her boots and headed for the door.

"Going somewhere?" he asked, chuckling as she startled and dropped her shoes.

"Oh!" She pressed her hands to her chest. "You scared me."

Wyatt swung his legs over the bed, stretching as he rose. "And where do you think you're off to?"

"Hospital," she said and bent to retrieve her boots. But not before she caressed him with her eyes and smiled.

"Without me?"

"What?"

"I thought I'd go with you." He slid on his jeans, the zipper hissing on its way up. Then he pulled his shirt on. His gaze wandered around the room looking for his socks.

"What?" she repeated.

He pronounced each word slowly. "You...me...together...hospital. Remember, your car is still at the bar."

"But you ride today." A bewildered expression drew her brows together into a thin line.

Threading his belt through the loops on his jeans, he casually said, "It's not a big deal. There will be other rodeos."

When his head rose, he was met with silence. Speechless, she stared at him as if he had lost his wits. She looked helpless, as if she were drowning in confusion.

He took a step toward her. "Lacy?"

Her outstretched palm stopped him. "N-no, you c-can't. I mean—I know how much this means to you."

A shower of light flooded the room as she flipped on the light switch. He squinted, eyes burning as they adjusted.

Hell, maybe she didn't want him to go with her. "Well, if you don't want me—"

"No—yes—it's just—you'd really choose my daughter over a rodeo?" Her face beamed, childlike, as if he'd offered her the world.

"Wouldn't anyone?" he asked, before he drew her into an embrace and kissed her forehead.

"No, not everyone," she muttered against his chest. She inched away from him. "I can't let you forfeit your rides. You go do your thing. After I speak with the doctor, and if Jessie is okay, maybe we can meet up later."

He held her at arms length. "Later? Are you sure?"

She nodded.

"How about I take you to get your car, then you can check on Jessie and swing by the rodeo grounds after?"

A frown bent her lips. She hesitated, seeming to struggle with the idea. After a moment she nodded her agreement, rose on her tiptoes, and kissed him tenderly.

"Thank you, Wyatt. Thank you for everything." Her words were soft and sincere.

He felt them pierce his heart like an arrow.

Chapter Nine

ဆ

Ace stirred nervously in the box. One of the horse's front hooves pawed the dirt as Wyatt crammed his fingers into tan leather gloves. From the booth in the middle of the arena, high above the crowd, he heard the announcer's introduction.

"Now give it up for a local cowboy right out of Chandler, Arizona, Wyatt Anderson. Hazing, Chance Mahan from Houston, Texas."

The black and white steer shot from the chute. Chance and Wyatt exploded out of the box, through the timing rope at the same time, one on each side of the animal. Immediately in position, Chance cut the steer right into Wyatt's path. Easy as slicing a hot knife through butter, Wyatt dropped on the steer, his feet bracing against the ground with a jolt.

Dirt clogged his nostrils as it rose around him. The familiar scents of his horse, the steer and his leather gloves penetrated the dusty film. A wisp of perspiration beaded his brow as he began to twist the steer's head.

The announcer's voice burst through the speakers with a cry of appreciation, "Yeah! Ladies and gentlemen, that's how it's done. Catch 'em right out of the chute," he said as the audience clapped and cheered.

"Did you see the way Wyatt pushed down on the inside horn and then dragged him down?" The announcer's voice paused in silent admiration. "This cowboy knows his stuff."

"Man, you must've had your Wheaties this morning." The clop of hooves followed Chance's gibe, as he approached Wyatt from behind. Ace snorted in agreement.

"4.2 seconds!" cried the announcer. The crowd went wild, shooting to their feet. Wyatt felt the heat of satisfaction rise up his neck as he looked into their cheering faces.

That was what made it all worthwhile—the satisfaction of a successful ride or event, and the accolades that followed from the overflowing stands of people.

There was nothing that compared.

A smile broke across Wyatt's face. "Without you—"

"Without me, you'da found some other lame-ass to take my place. Now let's get a beer. I'm buying."

Outside the arena they tied up their horses. Together they strolled to one of the refreshment stands advertising beer. The smells of barbeque and hamburgers cooking on an open grill filled the air. Wyatt's stomach growled. The last thing he needed was a beer on an empty stomach. But what the hell. This was probably his last rodeo. He might as well live it up.

Leaning against a post, Wyatt tipped the beer to his mouth. He wondered how Lacy's daughter was this morning.

"Gordon rode an eighty-two..." Chance's words mixed with Wyatt's thoughts of the trials Lacy was facing alone. How did one deal with the possibility of their child's death?

"...rode Cyclone..."

Last night, Lacy's tears and the desolate look in her eyes had torn at his heart.

"...I drew Madderhorn." Chance paused. "Wyatt? Are you listening to me?" Then the man's famous shit-eating grin curved his lips. "Only a woman could put that puppy

105

dog, I-miss-her-*sooo*-much expression on a man's face. You in love or just in lust?"

Wyatt gave Chance a playful shove.

"You didn't forget about Mad Dog, did ya buddy?"

"They're divorced, you imbecile." Wyatt chugged the remaining beer and tossed it in the trashcan.

"Divorced?" Chance ordered another round. "Well, you still watch your back. Mad Dog's not one to mess with." He pressed the cold one into Wyatt's palm. "From his familiarity with Lacy last night, he needs a reminder he's divorced. Hey, you guys left kinda early."

Wyatt tipped the bottle to his mouth. "Went to the hospital." He wiped his mouth with the back of his hand.

"What?" Chance pushed away from the side of the refreshment stand he leaned against and took several steps toward Wyatt. "Everything all right?"

"Lacy's daughter is ill."

Chance's surprise was evident in his raised voice. "Daughter?"

"It appears Mad Dog's a daddy."

They began to walk. The smell of dust rose in the air as a young woman galloped her horse through the crowd.

Chance smiled, his gaze pinned on the woman's ass as it rose from the saddle. "What's wrong with the girl?"

"Heart. Needs a transplant. Last night was a close one. Her blood pressure dropped."

Chance turned back around to Wyatt. "Man, I'm sorry. Lacy okay?"

Wyatt shrugged. "Don't know. One minute, yes, the next, no."

"Hell of a thing." Chance shook his head. "How old is she?"

"Don't know. In fact, I don't know a lot about Lacy and her daughter." It was true. They'd never really sat down and had a conversation. He didn't know where she was from, if she had family.

Nothing.

If it hadn't been for the events of last night, he wouldn't even know her last name, that she was divorced, or that she had a kid.

Somewhere between their brief encounters, they needed to talk, get to know each other better.

Then he grinned, thinking of the things he already knew about Lacy. She had a sensitive spot behind each ear. A light nuzzle or a soft kiss there sent tremors through her.

And her body. She had long luscious legs that fit tight around his hips when he rode her, and full breasts that tasted like honey on his tongue. His mouth watered just thinking about the other part of her anatomy that felt and tasted so good.

"Wyatt." A sharp nudge from Chance ripped Wyatt's memories from him. "Better wipe that horny look off your face. Don't want anyone thinking you're sweet on me." Chance dodged Wyatt's playful punch, as he staggered back laughing. "Man, she's got you tied in knots." Chance shook his head in disbelief. "Someone's finally roped the wild stallion."

Wyatt couldn't deny she'd tied him up in knots since the first time he'd laid eyes on her. It had been basic lust, not emotions—just out of control male hormones. But somewhere along the way it had changed, subtly, quickly, into…feelings, caring.

Wyatt shook his head attempting to shake the sappy thoughts away.

Man, Chance was right. He sounded like a boy with a crush. Schoolboy crush? No, he was a man with a serious hard-on for one woman.

Over the loudspeaker, Wyatt heard calf roping announced. Next would be bareback riding. Both Chance and Wyatt passed on a third beer for inspection of their gear as they headed for Wyatt's horse trailer.

"Toss me my rope." Chance held out a hand as Wyatt slung the coiled snake to him, his grasp falling short. The inaccuracy brought a frown to Chance's mouth.

"Thought you were a whiz with a rope," cajoled Wyatt.

A mischievous grin twisted Chance's lips. "Good with a rope? Well, maybe in the bedroom."

His friend's teasing brought up an image of Lacy tied to Wyatt's bed. His cock hardened. He couldn't help the ache that filled his balls. Man, what he wouldn't give to be inside that woman right now.

The cinch of Wyatt's rigging clanked against the side of the wooden trunk as he lifted it out of the tack storage compartment of his horse trailer. Rosin from the handgrip dusted his gloves. Wistfully, he looked at the bareback riggin' that had been part of him throughout the years. "After this weekend I'm retiring you," he muttered.

"What?" Chance asked, a frown furrowing his brow.

"After this weekend I'm retiring from bareback."

"Too old?" Chance snickered.

Wyatt thought a moment. Someday he'd get married, settled down, have kids.

Oddly, Lacy sprang to mind.

"Yeah, too old," Wyatt responded with a smile. It was time he entered into another phase of his life. One that didn't pose so much risk, at least to his body. But what about his heart?

The man on the other end of the loudspeaker announced the bareback riding would commence in ten minutes. Wyatt gathered his rigging and both he and Chance headed for the chutes.

Just Wyatt's luck, he had been chosen to ride first. Lightning was the name of the bronco he'd ended up with. He climbed up the side of the fence and eased onto the horse, then raised his hand.

The mare bolted out of the chute and then came to an abrupt halt, jarring Wyatt's teeth. All four of the horse's legs quivered as they planted firmly against the ground. Wyatt raked the gray's neck with his spurs.

"Buck, damn you," he cursed, wondering if the damn thing would move before the horn sounded. An eight second ride didn't leave much time to dazzle the judges, especially when the fuzztail decided it was better to wait out the clock than give the cowboy atop her a ride.

Just when Wyatt gave up hope, the horse jerked alive. In a brilliant display of orneriness, she tucked her hind legs to her belly, and then with a force that Wyatt thought would tumble him, the horse's legs shot high into the air. As the mare moved with lightning speed, Wyatt realized how she'd got her name.

The remainder of the time passed quickly as the mare jerked Wyatt forward and then with a whiplash sent him backward. The strain on his right hand and arm was unbearable as he fought to stay atop the bronco. When the buzzer finally blared, Wyatt was glad to see the pickup man heading his way.

It had been a rough start, but in the end, the crowd got their money's worth. Wyatt felt it in every muscle in his body. Yep, it was time to quit this foolishness.

Apprehensively, Lacy walked back into the life she thought she'd left behind. Rodeo was a thing of her past. She didn't miss it, she told herself as familiar sights and smells flooded over her—horses, cattle, cowboys, clowns, manure and the smell of leather.

God, she loved the smell of leather.

Memories bombarded her. Another time, another rodeo, where her life had taken a drastic one-eighty.

Barrel racing had been her sport. She'd been the best once. But love and an unexpected pregnancy had brought her career to a halt. Trophies and silver belt buckles were now dusty and packed away. They were all she had left. She'd even sold her horse to pay the bills.

Dust tickled Lacy's nose. She sneezed. Last night's rain hadn't made a dent in the dirt kicking up around her. Except for the occasional puddle here and there, no one would have known it had recently rained.

It wasn't a surprise that Lacy saw familiar faces. Rodeo was in the blood. These people were a rare bunch. A sense of melancholy overtook her as she recognized Cowboy Joe. Hunched and older now, he was dressed in his clown costume, leaning against a post. How many times had she seen that exact sight? Twenty years from now he'd still be there, leaning against a post, waiting for his turn to perform.

If a cowboy couldn't ride horses or bulls, he spent his time foolishly running to or from them, just to be a part of the circuit.

Sad. No, more than sad. It was heartbreaking.

Lacy glanced at her watch. It was five o'clock, she had to be at work by seven. It was her last night at High Country.

Sunday would be a day of rest. Then off to a new job on Monday. She glanced around, startled when she felt an arm slip around her waist.

"Hey, baby," said Jay, as he swung her around and into his arms. "You're late. You missed my ride."

"I didn't come to watch you ride," Lacy grunted, as she attempted to pull from his embrace.

"Why'd you come then? Is it Jessie?"

Lacy stopped her struggle and pinned him with a glare. "Jessie? Well, Jay, Jessie's in the hospital. Did you know that?" Red-hot anger simmered through her veins. "Did you know that she's on the heart transplant list? Third, possibly second on the list after last night's scare. Did you know that?" she screeched, her high-pitched voice tight and breathless.

Moisture filled her eyes. "Do you know what happens, Jay, if Jessie doesn't get a—" Lacy couldn't finished her sentence, the pain, the anger too great.

"Doll, just calm down," he placated, pulling her closer.

Lacy trembled with the uncontrollable urge to hit him. Her fingers curled into fists. "Calm down!? Get your fucking hands off me."

"Now, Lacy, you don't mean that."

Wyatt strolled around the corner and came to a stop. Lacy stood before him and her sonofabitch ex-husband had his arms wrapped around her again.

"What're you looking at?" Mad Dog hissed, his arms tightening around her waist.

"Lacy, you okay?" Wyatt asked, his fingers itching to wring the ignorant man's neck.

She frowned, continuing to push against the man's chest. "Fine, Wyatt."

Mad Dog glanced from Lacy then to Wyatt. A scowl twisted his features. "You fucking my wife?" His lips rose, baring his teeth in a snarl.

"Ex-wife, Jay. Remember?" She pushed at his hands, but they didn't move. "After I surprised you in Tulsa and found you elbows, knees and ass deep with that little rodeo queen."

"You'll always be mine, Lacy. And no one messes with my woman," he rumbled. Suddenly he pushed Lacy from his arms and swung.

Wyatt didn't have time to catch Lacy as she stumbled, but he was ready for the sucker punch. A bent arm blocked the man's right, while Wyatt's other fist returned a solid left to Mad Dog's jaw. There was a deep, hollow "ugh" as the man's feet flew out from under him sending him sprawling to the ground.

A surprised expression spread across Mad Dog's face as he lay in the dirt. Dazed, he rose into a sitting position, rotated his jaw and then touched it carefully.

"C'mon." Wyatt extended a hand to help Lacy off the ground. Then he slipped his arm around her shoulder. "Let's get out of here."

As they turned to walk away, contempt dripped from Mad Dog's lips. "You can't ride two stallions with one ass, Lacy."

The crude insinuation brought Wyatt to a sudden halt. Anger rushed across his face like a blazing inferno. Slowly, dangerously, he turned.

"Please, Wyatt. He's baiting you." Her trembling fingers clenched in the folds of his shirt. "Wyatt—"

A smirk crawled like a snake across Mad Dog's face. His hand wiped the blood trickling from the corner of his mouth as he stood. "Bring it on," he growled through a smirk. The fingers on his left hand curled in a come-and-get-me gesture.

But before a fight ensued, Chance and several of Wyatt's friends grabbed Mad Dog by his arms and dragged him backwards. Struggling, he howled like a trapped animal.

Wyatt took one step forward, when Lacy's hand stopped him. "Don't. It's not worth—"

Instead of continuing his pursuit of wiping the ground with Lacy's ex-husband, Wyatt drew her into his arms and silenced her with a blistering kiss.

Mad Dog's string of curses filled the air, then everything but Lacy's soft lips disappeared. When they finally broke apart, he couldn't remember where he was, only that his body had to feel hers naked beneath him, his cock buried deep inside her.

"C'mon." He grabbed her hand and led her away. Adrenaline and lust was a frustrating combination. His gaze scanned the many trucks and horse trailers looking for somewhere private, somewhere he could stake his claim on her, so she—as well as the arrogant ex—knew she was his.

From the corner of his eye he saw his truck and horse trailer. Sex in a horse trailer? Well, there was a first time for everything.

Okay, so it wasn't the most romantic place. Nonetheless, it was handy and he needed to work off some of the pent-up frustration begging for release. If Lacy was willing—it would have to do.

She cocked a brow as he opened the side door to the trailer and pulled her through.

From a cubbyhole, Wyatt extracted a wool horse blanket, shook it, and then spread it out on the floor of the trailer. It wasn't the softest thing, but it would be a barrier between skin and the wood planks.

Thankfully, Ace, his horse, hadn't dropped a load this morning. Other than the scent of horse and manure way past prime, and the sounds of the rodeo continuing around them, it was private.

The bewildered expression on Lacy's face almost made him laugh. Then realization dawned, and she smiled. Desire brightened her golden eyes.

His fingers slipped just beyond her belt, wedging between skin and material, as he tugged her toward him. "Okay, with you?"

Her tongue made a sensual path along her bottom lip. She nodded.

Both of them moved at once. His large fingers worked on the button of her tight pants. Each time he thought he had it, she'd move and it slipped through his fingers. She apparently wasn't having any more success than he, as she struggled to tug his shirt from his pants.

Almost as if they'd read each other's mind, they switched, focusing on their own clothing.

Her breathing matched his, heavy and fast. The need to touch her skin, feel her warm, wet flesh wrapped around his cock was unbearable.

Pants pooling around their boots, their eyes met. Simultaneously, they both broke into uncontrollable laughter.

His large hand cupped her bare ass and pressed her to his groin. "This isn't going to work, is it?"

She laid her head on his chest, releasing a frustrated sigh. Her hands grasped the cheeks of his butt, then stroked gently. "I don't think so."

"And there's another problem."

She looked up at him. "What?"

His mouth twisted into a frown. "No protection."

Lacy rolled her eyes and shook her head. Her sigh mimicked his disappointment, as well.

She took a step backward and stroked her palms up and down his arms. "I've got to go anyway. I work at seven o'clock. Are you coming over tonight?" Wyatt heard the longing in her voice.

He squeezed her tightly to him. "A stampede couldn't keep me away."

"Wyatt, don't come to High Country tonight," she murmured against his chest.

He held her at arms length. He read the concern in her furrowed brow. "Why?"

"Jay. I don't want any trouble."

He pulled her back into his arms, nuzzled the top of her head, inhaling the herbal scent of her shampoo. "Nothing will happen."

She pushed away from him, and bent to pull her pants up. "Please, Wyatt. Jay is possessive and easily riled."

Lacy had no idea what she was asking of him.

Wyatt watched her for a moment. Silently, he reached for his pants, pulling them up over his engorged erection. He rolled his hips, settling himself as comfortably as possible, before tucking his shirt into his pants. His zipper made a sharp sound as he raised it. Then he fastened his belt.

"Nothing will happen. By the way, how's Jessie?" And just like that he changed the subject.

Lacy grinned. "She's good. We watched a little TV. She loves SpongeBob. Then we played a game of Old Maid…"

Wyatt held the door open and followed her out. He heard Gordon's name called over the loudspeaker. The bull riding was finishing up.

"…before I knew it, it was four o'clock." Lacy glanced at her wristwatch. "Oh, I need to get going." She perched on tiptoe and pressed her lips briefly to his.

Wyatt's hands rose to circle her waist, but she stepped back out of his grasp.

"I'll see you tonight," she said, and then turned, leaving him in desperate need of a cold shower.

Chapter Ten

ꙅꙩ

The noise in the bar rose to a loud roar as Lacy sent a cowboy soaring through the air, then crashing into the mat. High Country was booming. And every drunken cowboy wanted a turn on the bull.

There was a rodeo dance in the center of the town plaza near Gilbert and Warner roads, but Lacy could swear everyone had evaded the town-sponsored event for High Country tonight.

Beer and whiskey flowed freely, as well as her tips. Her chest rose as she breathed in the rowdy crowd. Tips were the only thing she would miss about this place.

A grin crept across her face. This was her last night. Tomorrow, a new life started for her and Jessie.

Then her shoulders drooped.

Tomorrow would also be the last time she'd see Wyatt. He'd follow the circuit. Dallas, Texas, if she remembered correctly.

Mentally, Lacy chastised herself as another cowboy straddled the bull. She'd known this was coming. She shifted the controls to low, and the mechanical heap began to move. It was all her fault. Now she just had to suck it up, and go on with her life, because she wouldn't introduce another man into Jessie's life who thought Lacy's bedroom had a swinging door.

The thought and the anxiety it caused had her increasing the speed of the bull. She shifted her hand to the right and the cowboy flew to his left, landing with a deep thud. Eyes wide, he scrambled on hands and knees to get away from the chunk of steel that continued to spin.

It was hard enough explaining to a four-year-old why her father didn't live with them. But hiding the tears and pain each time Jay breezed through their lives had been the most difficult.

Not realizing that she'd already unsaddled the man, she flipped the switch and the mechanical bull swung to the left.

Hell, Jay had been in town for three days and hadn't made any attempt to see Jessie. He probably thought Lacy would ask for more money.

Her fingers tight on the controls, she increased the speed. The bull pulled to a stop and then sprang into action again.

"Lacy!" Mark yelling her name jerked her head up and brought her out of the pity party she was embroiled in. "You okay?" he asked.

The people around the bull pen silently stared at her. Embarrassed, she pushed away from the control table and rose. "Yeah, can you take over? I need a break." Without waiting for an answer, she began to blindly walk through the crowd and out the front door.

Lacy breathed in the cool night air and looked at the starry sky playing peekaboo through gray-blue clouds. When she hit the parking lot she stopped, leaning against a pickup. She closed her eyes thinking about Jessie, about Wyatt.

"Dreaming of me?" Wyatt's deep, seductive voice caressed her ears. She couldn't help the smile that tipped up the corners of her lips.

"No, don't open your eyes." She felt his body heat close in on her.

"Why?"

"Because I'm going to ravish you in this parking lot and I don't want anyone to see, including you." His words made her pulse jump.

"Wyatt?"

"Shhh." His warm breath flowed over her face. He smelled of soap and spicy aftershave.

Her tongue made an anxious path across her bottom lip.

When his large hands stroked the outside of her thighs, slowly raising her skirt, Lacy's breath hitched. She knew that she should stop him, that any moment someone could catch them, but there was something about this man that stripped her of all willpower. Even though she'd lose him tomorrow, she felt selfish, she wanted him tonight.

She pressed her back to the cold steel behind her and waited impatiently for his next move.

Wyatt tugged at her panties, pulling them off her hips, over her thighs, past her knees. When he nudged the heel of one of her boots, she lifted her foot. He did the same thing to her other foot and she was bare-assed.

She swallowed hard. "Wyatt?"

"Shhh." His hands returned to her thighs, stroking.

Air refused to enter her lungs. She couldn't breathe. Here she stood in a short skirt that barely covered her ass and now her pussy was bared, drenching her inner thighs with excitement. All she could think of was Wyatt's fingers and where she knew they would best fit.

"Do you want me to touch you?" His question slid like a soft feather over her skin, teasing and arousing.

She opened her mouth and a strangle sound emerged. Her nipples had beaded into painful nubs. Her thighs parted on their own accord. She needed him.

The devil chuckled. "I'll take that as a yes."

Calloused hands burned a path of fire up her inner thighs, pressing her wider for his exploration. Thumbs massaged her pelvic bones through her thatch of curly hair.

Her knees buckled, her body dipped. Her bones felt like rubber and refused to hold her upright as she waved her hands blindly through the air to hold onto him. "Wyatt?"

Before she knew it, she was in his arms. She could hear his labored breathing, feel the rapid rise and fall of chest.

"Don't open your eyes." He twisted her around, so that she felt the truck beneath her hands.

Was he going to enter her from behind? The thought sent another flow of desire seeping down her thighs.

He raised her hands and curled her fingers around the truck's door handle. "Hold on, I'll be right back." Gravel crunched as he moved away.

Creak. Thud. Lacy heard the familiar sounds of a tailgate being opened. *Uh-oh.* A delightful tingle stung her nipples. Within a second Wyatt was back, his strong arms lifting her off the ground. He took several steps, the cool air stroking her wet pussy. She shivered, thinking that someone might approach and the first thing they'd see was her pussy glowing in the moonlight. Talk about excitement—just the thought made her pulse race.

Then she gasped as the back of her thighs, her ass and her swollen folds met cold steel. The man had set her on the tailgate.

"Wyatt?"

"Lord, woman, can you be quiet? I need to concentrate."

"Concentrate? Do you have any idea what this is doing to me? And I hope this is your truck," she added.

He grabbed her hand. The next thing she knew she was cupping his erection. It was hard and thick, straining against his jeans.

"Does that answer your question? And yeah, it's my truck," he said, his tone deep and strained.

Her palm stroked his flesh through the denim. A fingernail scraped the metal zipper, gripping the clasp and slowly dragging it down.

The music from the band playing inside the bar was beginning to fade. Instead, crickets sang a serenade. The soft purr of engines as traffic passed in the distance seemed louder, closer. God, she couldn't believe she was allowing him to fuck her in High Country's parking lot.

As her fingers slipped between the folds of his jeans, he pressed his hips forward. "Ah, Lacy." His voice was a throaty growl.

As she grasped him, she realized he didn't have any briefs on. "No briefs?"

"Nothing to get in the way of what I have planned." His words held a wealth of promise that had her splaying her legs as he slipped from her grasp and crouched down before her. "Thatagirl."

Pebbles popped underneath his boots. Then she felt his warm tongue press against her sex. "Wyatt!"

"Shhh, I skipped dessert tonight. Thought I'd have a bite." His words echoed through her body and she was lost.

She raised her skirt around her waist and spread her legs wider. "Bon appétit," she whispered as she leaned back, resting on the palms of her hands.

He growled as his mouth pressed against her heat and his tongue pierced her pussy. His thumbs held her wide, giving him access to the soft flesh. He tasted her, making groans that excited and thrilled her.

He nipped her clit. She squealed, coming off the tailgate and landing hard. He anchored her by cramming his hands up her shirt and grasping a breast in each palm. Pinching her sensitive nipples, he went back to work, laving and sucking and biting.

An explosion burst inside the center of her core. Her fingers grabbed handfuls of his hair, smothering his face between her thighs as she rode the wave of her climax. His tongue met each thrust of her hips as he feasted on her juices. He growled and she felt the vibration echo through her body, adding to the sensations sending her into meltdown. The thought that someone might be watching made each shimmer of ecstasy intensify.

When the last of the spasms were wrung from her body, she released the death-grip she had on his head.

"My turn." His voice was husky. "Open your eyes."

Lacy was almost afraid to. What if this was only a dream? She didn't want it to end, not now, not tonight, not ever. Slowly her eyelids rose.

The depths of desire in his eyes as he crushed his mouth to hers was breathtaking. The heady taste and scent of her arousal assaulted her senses as he jabbed his tongue between her lips. Her flavor was on his face, his lips, in his mouth—turning her on, edging her closer to another summit. Hell, before the night was over she'd make her mark on every inch of his delicious body.

Then his hands left her and she felt him release the button keeping his pants together. When he moved between her legs her folds parted. He reached in his pocket, extracting a condom. He fumbled with the package.

"Now," she groaned, wanting to feel him sliding deep inside her.

Lacy's breathing was as jerky and uneven as his, when she adjusted her hips and took his cock inside her. She wiggled against him and he thought he'd die. He couldn't believe that they were having sex in a parking lot, on the tailgate of his truck. But damn, it was a turn-on. He was on the verge of coming when she flexed her inner muscles and clamped down on his throbbing cock.

"Lacy—no—dammit—don't move," he ordered desperately, his hands tightening on her hips, trying to hold her still while he fought to gain control. Her body refused to obey as she bucked under him.

His toes nearly curled in his boots. "What the hell," he cursed, pulling out then plunging deep, filling her completely.

Wide-eyed, she cried out, her body arching off the tailgate. She was so hot and tight and ready for him. Her pussy contracted, pulsed, and then a shiver shook her. The spasms of pleasure seemed to go on forever, milking him, pulling him deeper.

Her nails raked across his shoulders, dragging a blazing path down his back. His hands smoothed across her hips to cup her buttocks, lifting and tilting them as a final plunge shoved him over the edge. The walls of her sex convulsed around him, squeezing every last bit of his seed from him. A shiver raked his spine and his cock jerked one last time.

Man, he hated condoms. He wanted to feel the leather when he rode. But better safe than sorry. But one day he would have her—all of her.

When he pulled away from her, she moaned in protest, reaching for him. Eager to resume their loving...until a truck rolled into the parking lot.

Shit. She pushed at his chest, pulling her skirt down as her feet hit the ground. It was all he could do to force his semihard cock back into his pants. He quickly zipped his pants and moved in front of Lacy to shield her from the strangers' eyes.

When he looked over his shoulder in the direction of the truck, recognition hit. It was Chance's pickup. He watched as his friend parked, then exited the vehicle, Rosy in tow.

God, how he wanted to knock the grin off Chance's face. Thankfully, his buddy didn't make a comment, but his woman did.

The redhead stopped in front of Wyatt. Her gaze moved up and down his length. "Nice ass," she purred as Chance grabbed her hand and pulled her along.

Lacy's body stiffened at the woman's giggles. "They saw," she gasped.

Wyatt stroked her arm. Her skin was cool to the touch, but damp from their loving. "Honey, all they saw was my bare ass."

"What?"

He squeezed her arm. "It's nothing, Lacy, just let it go."

Her eyes widened. "Wyatt, we're not two horny teenagers. We're adults who just got caught screwing in a parking lot."

He wiggled his brows up and down. "Fun, wasn't it?"

"Ohhhh…" She jerked her arm out of his grasp. Then he saw the spark in her eyes and the smile that surfaced. "Look what you do to me. Where are my panties?" She scanned the ground.

Wyatt slipped the silky bikinis from his pocket and waved them in front of her face. As she lunged for them he crammed them back into his pocket.

"You're not going to wear any panties tonight."

"What?" Her voice hit a new high.

"Tonight when I catch you in the hall, or when no one's looking, I want to touch you. Not a scrap of material, but *you*."

She dove toward his pocket. His outstretched palm landed against her shoulder, halting her.

"Wyatt, I can't."

"You can and you will, for me."

"Oh God." Her chest rose and fell rapidly. For a moment, Wyatt wondered if she would hyperventilate. Then she squared her shoulders, took a deep breath. "Only if I can do the same. No hiding behind a zipper. Before you touch me I have to be able to freely touch you. Deal?" She jutted her hand out.

This woman was amazing. Wyatt clasped her hand and shook it. "Deal."

"Now, I've got to get back to work."

Wyatt slipped his arm around her waist as they began to walk toward the bar's entrance. His hand floated down to her ass, then slipped beneath her skirt.

She jerked her hips. "No cheating." She grinned and dodged him.

Tonight was going to be hell.

The sway of Lacy's hips, the way she leaned against the post as she gave Larry her order, her skirt inching upward, made Wyatt achingly hard. Who knew that knowing a woman didn't wear panties would make him as randy as stallion in a corral full of mares?

And damned if the woman didn't know it too.

Her seductive movements were for him, but he wasn't the only man watching her. Several had copped a feel, shooting him from his chair like an arrow from a bow. She always had it under control before he approached.

Wyatt crammed his hand in his pocket to feel the silk of her panties slipping through his fingers. That alone made him rock-hard. He thought of returning her panties, but when she winked at him from across the room and ducked down a hall, his heart crashed against his chest. He stood, anticipation hastening his steps.

Quietly, he closed the door behind him, noting there wasn't a lock, but his gaze was diverted by the woman sitting on a stack of beer crates. One leg dangled, the other bent at the knee, boot propped up so her delicious pink folds were eagerly displayed.

Lacy cocked a brow and pointed to his crotch. "Down, boy. All the way to your boots."

He turned back to the door. "No lock."

"Forget it. If we get caught we get caught," she purred.

Fuck. She was going to kill him. Just the thought of someone walking in on them made him harder than a rock. As he approached, his fingers tugged at the zipper that took this inopportune time to stick. He looked down at the metal refusing to budge and then back at the woman tapping her watch lightly.

"Shit." He struggled until the zipper gave. His pants were down around his boots in no time.

When he reached for her, she stopped him with an outstretched palm. Then she removed his hat setting it beside her. "Wait. There's something I've been wanting to do." She slipped off the stack of beer. As she sank to her knees, Wyatt held his breath.

Golden eyes gazed up at him. Then she grasped his ass and pulled him to her.

A breath caught in his throat as her mouth, hot and wet, wrapped around his firm, unsheathed cock. Her tongue stroked the tip and a tremor raked his spine.

She moaned and he thrust his hips, burying himself deep. She took all of him, while her palm cupped his sac, kneading gently.

It was hard for Wyatt to breathe. His heart pounded against his chest as if it would burst at any moment. Electricity pulled from the base of his erection to the tip. A groan squeezed from his lips.

This was every man's dream, a scene straight out of the dark fantasies buried deep in his mind. His eyes were pinned to the beautiful woman kneeling before him. She was his. If he asked, would she indulge *all* his fantasies? The thought made his erection jerk against the inside of her cheek.

Wyatt sucked in a breath through clenched teeth watching his cock slide in and out of her full lips. She watched him through dark eyes. When his nostrils flared, she sucked harder.

His eyes drifted closed and he allowed himself to simply feel the exquisite touch of her tongue tracing the underside of his cock. She was tight, wet and warm. Her teeth scraped him several times, gently.

As fire radiated down his erection, his eyes popped open, his body clenching. "Whoa, baby." He attempted to ease out of her mouth, but her hands were melded to his ass. "Stop, Lacy, or I'll spill in your mouth."

She released him, lolling back on her calves as she wiped her mouth with the back of her hand.

"Come here." She took his offered hand and he pulled her to her feet. Hands around her waist, he raised her off her feet and settled her back on the stack of beer.

He reached into his pocket and extracted a condom. His hands trembled as he slid the cool prophylactic over his aching flesh. It felt tighter than normal. Without hesitating, he moved between her thighs.

Flexing her hips against him, she clasped her palms on his lower back, tugging him to her.

When his cock slid into her pussy, Lacy tensed, fighting back the climax that hovered within her. He was so large, so hot, that it felt like a branding iron seared her body. The feeling was so exquisite, she wanted to hang from the precipice as long as she could. If he moved, she'd be a goner.

Evidently, he stood on the same threshold, as he remained motionless. Yet, the flame of desire still raged within his dusky-blue eyes.

"If I move, I'll lose it." His voice was hoarse, strained.

She laughed, her muscles inadvertently squeezing him. He growled, thrust forward, and she felt the jerks of his cock as he exploded. Like a chain reaction, the climax of a lifetime ripped through her body. It was like a brushfire raging through her body, her clit became so sensitive rubbing against him, that she cried out—lost somewhere between pain and pleasure.

Wyatt's palm covered her mouth, muffling the scream. The tense expression on his face revealed his own difficulty remaining silent.

When her orgasm subsided and logical thought returned, she pressed her head to his shoulder.

His arms wrapped around her. He rested his chin on her head. "I thought having you once would be enough. Instead, I need you more each time."

Lacy couldn't restrain the delight she felt. "You do?" Then the moment slipped away, leaving in its place a big helping of skepticism.

Sweet talk. That was all it was. *You'll desire me until you have to leave.* Which, she reminded herself, was tomorrow. The burst of energy drained away, leaving her feeling sad and empty.

Lacy fought the prickle of tears burning behind her eyelids. Her head still lay against Wyatt's chest and she inhaled, attempting to embed the spicy masculine scent that was his alone into her memory banks. In the future, during the restless nights when she lay alone, she could conjure up his face, his taste and scent.

"I need to get back to work." She banished the unshed tears from her voice.

He stepped back, hands on her waist as he helped her down from the cartons. Lacy could feel the impression of the crates on her ass, as she shimmied her skirt back into place.

His hand brushed a stray piece of her hair away from her eyes. "Do you want me to wait for you, or pick something up to eat and meet you at your house?"

"Wyatt, could we pass on tonight? I'm feeling a little tired."

He beamed. "Wore you out?"

She forced a weak smile. "Yeah." She turned her back to him, trying to keep her composure and not fall to pieces in front of him.

The sound of him righting himself was like the slamming of a door between them.

Lacy wasn't good at goodbyes, and this one felt like a knife to her gut.

How could she have fallen for this man in such a short period of time? She swallowed hard.

He moved behind her, his body spooning hers. He pressed a kiss to the top of her head. "Okay, honey. Will you be at the rodeo tomorrow? You haven't seen me ride."

She could hear the pride and excitement in his voice. "No, I need to spend the day with Jessie."

He tensed against her back. "But I leave for Texas right after I ride."

The pain was unbearable. It was happening again. Another man was leaving her to chase the rodeo. She blinked at the tears gathering in her eyes, thankful he couldn't see them.

How many times had she gone through this scene with Jay?

There was real disappointment in his voice when he finally spoke. "I understand. I'll call or see you when I get back in town."

Oh, if she only had a dollar for every time she'd heard that one.

"Sure." She broke out of his arms and headed toward the door at a fast pace. She brushed her hand through the air, and glanced over her shoulder. "See ya."

Pushing open the storage room door, she exited, making a beeline to the ladies restroom before the dam she held back burst. She barely made it into a stall before the first tear fell.

Wyatt inhaled, tucking his shirt into his pants and grabbing his hat. What a hell of a night. He exited through the door Lacy had left wedged open. She was amazing. His gaze scanned the hall looking for her.

He had been looking forward to waking in her arms tomorrow morning. His fingers threaded through his hair, before he planted his hat squarely back on his head. Well, there'd be other nights — plenty of them.

Lacy was nowhere to be found as he looked around the packed bar. Chance waved from the dance floor and Wyatt gave him a nod. It was getting late. Maybe he'd call it a night as well. He scanned the bar again for Lacy, wanting to see her one more time before he left.

Hell, the meeting in Houston was only for two days. He'd be back Tuesday night. Surely he could stand to be away from the woman for that length of time.

Chapter Eleven

℘

There was nothing like waking to the smell of damp feathers. Lacy pushed her tear-drenched, goose down pillow away from her face and inched her body into a sitting position. It was Sunday and already it felt like a lifetime since she'd last seen Wyatt.

"Shit, Lacy, you'll never make it through the day, much less the rest of your life, thinking like that." The words were right, but the tone reflected how she really felt inside. Hopeless and empty.

The clock on the bed stand flashed ten o'clock. She'd overslept. Wyatt was probably already at the rodeo arena. In less than eight hours he'd be down the road and out of her life.

"For heavens sake, Lacy." She pushed herself off the bed, stood and caught her reflection in the mirror. It looked like a southbound train had left tracks across her face. Her mascara was smeared. Her eyes were red and swollen. And her face resembled a puffer fish.

No winning beauty contests for her today.

She headed for the bathroom to wash away the evidence of her grief. The cool washcloth felt good on her face. She left it over her eyes longer than was necessary, an excuse to delay facing the day. When she had enough of her pity party, she tossed aside the rag, pushed away from the sink and headed to the bedroom to get dressed.

The ride to the hospital was uneventful until she exited her car, slamming the locked door with her keys still in the ignition.

Her shoulders fell, a heavy sigh pushing from her tight lips.

"Damn. What's *this* going to cost?" If this was her new life, it sure wasn't starting off on the right foot. Maybe one of the orderlies would be able to use a clothes hanger to squeeze through her window and unlock the door. It was either that, or fork out some much-needed dough to have a locksmith come to the hospital — on a Sunday, to boot.

Lacy needed a plan. It was already formulating by the time she reached Jessie's door and pushed it open. Her feet came to an abrupt stop. Her daughter was surrounded by stuffed animals.

Jessie's wide eyes greeted her. "Mommy, look." Her tiny voice was filled with awe.

Lacy picked up a purple bear, set it down, and picked up a beautiful white unicorn with a golden horn. "Where did these come from?"

"Daddy," Jessie squealed with glee.

Lacy's heart dropped to the floor. "He was here?"

Jessie clung to a doll with auburn hair to match her own. "Uh-huh. He's coming home."

Lacy's pressed her shaky palm over her mouth.

What now? How was she to handle this?

As anger heated her face, she blurted, "Why can't he just stay away?"

Jessie's face wrinkled. Tears moistened her eyes. "Mommy," her voice trembled.

Lacy rushed to her daughter's side. Sitting on the side of the bed, she cradled Jessie in her arms. "I'm sorry, baby. Shhh, don't cry."

Jessie's shoulders shook through her tears. "Can he come home?"

Damn the man.

Lacy brushed a lock of hair from Jessie's face. Smiling as brightly as she could, Lacy asked, "Did your daddy want you to ask me if he could come home?"

Jessie nodded. "It's a secret. Don't tell."

Lacy's teeth ground together. By the grace of God, she withheld the fury building inside her. She blinked back hot tears beating like fists against her eyelids. "Not a word, baby," she choked. "I promise."

Lacy had wondered why the asshole hadn't shown his lowlife face at High Country last night. Now she knew. He had been bribing their daughter to weasel his way back into their lives.

Blinking back unshed tears, Jessie asked, "Can he, Mommy?"

The last thing Jessie needed was to become upset. But what was Lacy supposed to say?

"Did he tell you he was leaving town today?"

Jessie nodded. "Uh-huh."

"Then why don't we wait until he comes back to discuss this. In the meantime, who's ready for a game of cards?"

Hell, she would rather play Old Maid with her daughter, than the game her ex-husband had just instigated.

As if Lacy wasn't dealing with enough, Jay had opened another can of worms. When she got her hands on the slimeball she'd give him a piece of her mind.

On Monday morning Wyatt pushed his chair closer to the huge conference table. Houston, Texas was their company's headquarters. It was always a perk to hobnob with the company elite, but not today. He looked around the spacious conference room while slipping his business jacket back on. Nice room, but it was colder than a northern breeze.

Wyatt felt like crap. He'd woken wanting Lacy in his arms. Sunday had been hell, but the next two days he was certain would be worse.

Wyatt shuffled through his notes for the umpteenth time. Across the table, one of his operations managers frowned. Carl Sanchez handled research and development. Not the typical pocket-protector engineer, he was a well-balanced manager who got the job done.

Next to him was John Chaney. John was a short, beefy man who handled new product introduction. His jolly attitude and sharp wit fit right in with the group at Dunbar Semiconductors.

Both were dressed in blue suits and white shirts. The only difference was their ties. Funny, but you could tell a lot about a man by his tie. Carl's was neat, tied to perfection, while John's was a little loose and off center, just like their personalities.

A vibration beat against Wyatt's waist as his cell phone went off. He reached to still the pain-in-the-ass thing. Setting it before him, he flipped open the lid.

What's up with you? The text message was from Carl.

Wyatt punched in a reply. *Nothing.* Then he set the cell on the table.

The little gray rectangle in front of him went off like a vibrator, moving across the surface of the table. He trapped it with his hand, popped the cover.

It was John this time. *You seem antsy. Weekend go bad?*

Again, Wyatt punched in a response, but this time sending it to both his managers. *Are you two paying attention to the presentation?*

In unison the men across the table from him opened their cell phones. Like puppets controlled by strings, their heads rose together and they glanced at each other, then at Wyatt.

Wyatt pinned them with a steely glare. A single brow rose. He regretted taking his frustration with himself out on the guys. He'd neglected to get Lacy's telephone number before leaving town. He'd called information, but no Lacy Mason was listed.

He punched in one last message to his staff. It read, *Sorry.*

Actually, his weekend couldn't have been better. He'd met the woman of his dreams. She was everything he wanted. Not to mention that sex with her was mind-blowing. He felt like his life had new direction.

Hell, he'd even taken second in steer wrestling.

Furthermore, he'd been wrong. He couldn't live several days apart from her. She was constantly on his mind, in his dreams. This morning he'd woken with a hard-on that a pole-vaulter could have used to clear a horizontal bar.

Even now he saw her face on every woman at the table. His hand skimmed across the polished table, the wood cool to his touch. The thought of the golden highlights in her hair made his cock twitch. His hips squirmed. He could almost feel her warm, wet folds cradling him.

He licked his lips, remembering the taste of her as he'd feasted on her woman's flesh. The palms of his hands itched to feel her silky hair, her satiny skin.

Wyatt glanced at his watch. Nine o'clock. This was going to be a helluva long day.

Lacy glanced at her watch, nine o'clock exactly. Okay, so she was on time, but where was Joy Thomas, the human resources manager?

The waiting room was filled with people either waiting to apply for a job, or attending orientation as she was.

She played with the hem of her skirt, hoping it wasn't too short, too wrinkled, or too navy blue. She'd passed up the red shirt for a soft pastel. The red probably would have given a *don't mess with me* impression. She wasn't sure what the light blue shirt said. Probably, *I'm scared witless by the amount of perspiration in my armpits.*

Then a young man sat down beside her. A spicy scent arose — Wyatt's cologne. The man smiled and Lacy forced herself to return the gesture.

She'd dreamed of Wyatt last night. The feel of his hands caressing her body, his warm, wet mouth teasing her nipples while his hard cock stroked in and out of her pussy…the dream had left her weary. Her cold shower had only made her uncomfortable, but hadn't dowsed the flame that burned inside.

It was nine-thirty when Lacy looked at her watch again. So, this was what it was going to be like working for Dunbar Semiconductors. Hurry up and wait.

"Lariat Mason." An older woman with reading glasses perched on her thin nose approached.

Lacy stood. She wiped her hands on her skirt. This was it.

The woman jutted her right hand out. "I'm Joy Thomas. Welcome to Dunbar Semiconductors." The greeting was extended with as much warmth as a melting ice cube.

Lacy's stomach growled.

The woman looked down her nose at Lacy. "No breakfast?"

Lacy felt like a child about to be schooled on the advantages of a healthy breakfast. "Nerves," Lacy admitted.

"Tsk, tsk, nothing to be nervous about." Ms. Thomas thick-heeled shoe squeaked as she turned and began to stroll away.

Lacy hesitated. Was she to follow?

The gray topknot on the woman's head faltered as she glared over her shoulder. "Ms. Mason, are you coming?"

Lacy stumbled in her haste to catch up.

The woman lifted a brow. Her nose raised an inch higher.

Man, this was tougher than Lacy had thought it would be. And she hadn't even met the people she'd be working with.

Lacy was led into a conference room filled with other people joining the company. Ms. Thomas stood in front of the room and with a scratchy voice welcomed everyone.

Two hours later, after watching a film on cleanroom techniques and an introduction by the CEO, she sat filling out numerous papers, including W-4s and other employment forms.

At last she stood in front of what Connie, the administrative assistant, referred to as Lacy's cubicle. A small four-by-five space with one chair, one computer, one stapler and one telephone. Cozy... *Not*!

"Carl was called to a meeting in Houston. He said to *welcome* you. Welcome. He won't be back until Thursday." Was Connie reading from an invisible script in front of her? Or had the introduction of new employees become old hat to this woman? "If you open the flipper to your right you'll find a number of items—procedures, rules, mottos. You need to review them."

Lacy just stood there like a bump on a log. "Flipper?"

Connie's snicker contained enough haughtiness to make Lacy's skin crawl. "You newbies. *Flipper*—the cabinet door." She shook her head and opened the door to a cabinet above the computer. "You'll find pens, paper, etcetera, in the other flipper—uh, cabinet. Filing cabinets are behind your chair."

Duh! I knew that.

As Connie shuffled out into the aisle, she tossed over her shoulder, "If you need anything, don't hesitate to ask."

Yeah. Right.

Overwhelmed, Lacy sat quietly for a moment to gather her wits. She had thought being a cocktail waitress was a tough job.

"Hi," a small voice came from over the wall. Lacy jumped when a dark head popped up over the five-foot barrier.

"Jumpy, huh? Wait a minute." The young woman's head disappeared. There were sounds of movement, a chair scraping across carpet, soft footsteps, then a petite woman sauntered into Lacy's cubicle.

"Hi, I'm Wendy Patterson, Planning." She extended a hand.

Lacy wouldn't call the woman pretty, but she had a pleasant demeanor. Thankful to see a friendly face, she accepted the woman's hand. "Lariat Mason. I believe Connie called me a newbie."

"Ahh, fresh out of college." Wendy chuckled.

"Ohhh…"

Wendy looked at the stacks of paper in Lacy's cabinets and frowned. "So it's the old baptism by fire."

"Excuse me?"

"You know. The old 'throw her in the deep end and see whether she sinks or swims'." Wendy made swiping movements with each arm like she was swimming.

"Carl is in Houston—"

"So Connie left you high and dry." She leaned toward Lacy. "I'll let you in on a little secret. Watch your back with Connie. Most of the people here are pleasant enough. The managers are great, but that one…" She shook her head. "Dangerous."

This was getting better by the minute.

"Don't mind me. I've been burned by her too many times. You need to make up your own mind. Anyway, let me give you a tour of our little home away from home."

"Home" consisted of a complex with four different buildings, each abutting a huge parking lot with tanks of compressed air, gases and numerous other chemicals. In one building was the credit union, another held the cafeteria, and still another contained human resources.

There were so many aisles branching off in so many directions that Lacy was afraid if she wandered off alone she would be lost for days before someone found her.

Thankfully the floor she worked on had a room that contained a refrigerator, a microwave and a coffee machine. Coffee was five dollars a week. The rules posted on the refrigerator said, *I'm not your mother. Clean up your own mess.* It was signed Connie.

Wendy introduced her to so many people that names and faces were a blur. Thank God for the badges everyone wore.

By noon, Lacy's head hurt and she hadn't even touched the tall stack of papers.

She started to sit down in her chair, but missed. The arm twisted so it wedged up her butt. When Wendy popped her head over the wall, Lacy scrambled to push the irritating armrest out of the way and fell into the chair with a thud.

"I hate those things, don't you?" Wendy didn't wait for an answer. "Lunch—you game?"

Lacy frowned at the pile of reading in front of her. "Yeah, I'm game." She rose, sticking her tongue out at the taunting stack of paper.

Thankfully, Wendy offered to drive. Her classy little red Spider left Lacy envious as they pulled into the Denny's parking lot.

As Wendy stepped from her car she asked, "Married?"

Lacy wasn't comfortable talking about her personal life. She hesitated, "No."

"Ah, divorced."

Lacy's eyes narrowed. "How did you know?"

Wendy held the door open and Lacy passed through. "You had that, *hell, no* look. C'mon." She pushed past the waitress and took a booth by the window, so they could watch the traffic.

The woman was an aggressive little thing, but Lacy liked her.

Wendy looked over the top of her menu. "So, any kids?"

A smile crept across Lacy's face. "A daughter, Jessie. She's four."

"Boyfriend?"

Yeah, for a whole weekend. "No."

The corners of the woman's mouth tugged downward. "Yeow! You'll have the men sniffing at your heels."

"Not likely. I'm not interested in men." Lacy raised her water glass to her mouth.

Wendy cocked a brow. "Lesbian?"

A stream of water gushed from Lacy's mouth, and before she could stop the flow it sprayed from her nose. She covered her nose and mouth, choking in embarrassment.

"I'll take that as a no." Wendy laid her menu down as the waitress in brown shorts and a white shirt approached their table. "A burger and fries. My friend here needs a napkin, and..."

"Soup. I'll take a bowl of soup." Lacy's stifled voice came out in a squeak.

The airport buzzed with travelers coming and going from Houston's Hobby Airport. Computers were down. Check-in was manual, which meant that all the flights leaving at 6:00 p.m. wouldn't leave until around 8:30 p.m. Not exactly what Wyatt had planned for his Wednesday evening. The meetings had lasted a day longer than he'd expected.

Carl, John and Wyatt stood in line for two hours before an attendant finally waved him to her. The robust black woman frowned when all three approached.

"Connected at the hip, or are y'all going to the same place?"

So much for customer service. Wyatt was in no mood for a smartass. "We're traveling together, destination Sky Harbor, Phoenix, Arizona."

An appreciative eye scanned him up and down. "So, pretty boy, you a desert rat?"

John and Carl chuckled behind him. Wyatt wasn't sure whether to strangle the offensive attendant or his staff members first.

He plopped his ID on the counter and pinned the attendant with a hot glare. "Phoenix," he said firmly.

She got the message. She didn't speak another word and processed not only his ticket, but John's and Carl's as well.

When the plane finally took off it was 9:30 p.m. Wyatt was tired and all he wanted was a warm shower and his bed. He laid his head back on the headrest, inched his seat back and settled in for the flight home.

He had wanted to stop by High Country and see Lacy tonight, but he was in a sour mood. Better to see her tomorrow.

An elbow nudged Wyatt and he opened his eyes. While John punched numbers into his computer, Carl wanted to talk.

"Did I tell you we had several newbies who joined us Monday?"

Wyatt exhaled slowly. "No."

Carl leaned back in his seat. "One of them is a looker, real eye candy."

Wyatt wasn't interested. A good-looking woman meant trouble in the workplace. He had enough problems trying to keep everyone happy in his department.

But Wyatt could see that Carl had more to say. "And?"

"And I just thought I'd mention it." A grin slid across Carl's face.

"I don't need to send you to another sexual harassment seminar, do I?" Last month Wyatt's entire staff had taken the online version of "Harassment in the Workplace". The damn class had reduced productivity and put everyone on edge.

"No." Then Carl quickly added, "But wait 'til you see her. I interviewed her in November with the other engineering students from ASU."

"Carl, have you forgotten that we hire engineers for the size of their brains, not their breasts?"

Carl grinned. "Oh, she's got 'em both. You'll be impressed. I've decided to allow her to work on the Sandric project with Tom."

Wyatt showed his disapproval with a frown. "Sandric?" Sandric was a developmental project for a small sensing device that would monitor acceleration and braking in a vehicle's brake system. Wyatt laid back his head, closing his eyes. "I hope you know what you're doing."

The last thing Wyatt needed was another woman confusing him. Lacy had embedded herself into his personal life. He didn't need another woman messing with his business life.

Chapter Twelve

As Lacy steered her Escort into the parking lot of Dunbar Semiconductors, she smiled. It was Thursday, the day her new boss, Carl, was due back from Texas. She was excited and a little apprehensive. He had made several telephone calls asking how she was settling in and whether she needed anything.

Either he was a nice, concerned manager or she was going to have problems. Lacy prayed for nice and concerned as she slammed the car door and headed for the revolving doors.

Crap. She'd left her badge in her car. As she turned to go back, Wendy stepped out of her shiny red Spider. She waved and Lacy returned the gesture. When the woman didn't take another step toward the entrance, Lacy assumed she was waiting on her. Quickly she unlocked her car, scrambling through the many things piled on the passenger seat. It was a miracle she located her badge as quickly as she did. Then she hastened toward Wendy.

As Lacy approached, Wendy flashed a warm smile. "Today's the big day, right? Meeting your boss?"

"Yeah, I'm a little nervous."

"Carl's nothing to worry about." She waved a dismissive hand through the air. "Now, David Anderson, that's another story."

"The VP?" Lacy remembered seeing his name outside the door where Crystal, the other administrative assistant, sat. Not to mention, his name was plastered on every piece of paper she had read.

"Yeah, the man's a heartthrob, if I've ever seen one. Strait laced, though. Never heard any rumors of him doing any of the staff, and it hasn't been because the ladies haven't tried. Hell, most of them would drop their drawers in a heartbeat, me included."

Lacy thought this type of talk was a bit inappropriate. Wendy didn't mean any harm—she was just being Wendy. But it did bring to mind another man Lacy thought was a heartthrob. Where was Wyatt now? Did he ever think about her?

In silence, they walked down the hall.

"You're awful quiet. You okay?" Wendy asked.

"Just anxious, I guess." Hell, that was an understatement. Her palms were sweating and her pulse was racing.

Wendy stopped, drawing Lacy to a halt. "Well, gather your courage, because Carl's headed our way."

Carl Sanchez was exactly how Lacy remembered him from her interview. A Hispanic man in his early thirties, pleasant enough looking, with a broad smile and chocolate brown eyes. He was probably three inches taller than her five-eight.

"Lariat," he called out as he approached. "Good to see you again." He pumped her hand like the handle to a water well. "Wendy, how's the cat?" he said without looking at the woman, his eyes fixed on Lacy.

"*Purr*-fect." Wendy cocked a brow. "How's the wife?"

Carl's face flushed. "Tina's good."

"The kids?"

"Good." The man shuffled his feet.

Boy was Wendy subtle, as subtle as a Mack truck.

Wendy winked at Lacy. "Well, I'll leave you two. I'm sure you have a lot to talk about."

Carl jerked his head to the right. "Join me for a cup of java in the cafeteria, I'm buying."

Lacy said what any new employee would as she began to follow him, "I'd love to."

Seven-thirty in the morning and the place was packed with people. A normal workday began at eight o'clock, but everyone seemed to be getting an early start. As they walked into the entrance of the cafeteria the smell of frying bacon met her nose, mixed with the strong, overpowering scent of garlic. To the left was the grill, to the right, chickens on a spit turned, their juices bubbling as preparations for lunch were already in the works.

"Donut?" Carl reached in and grabbed a raised donut with chocolate icing from a shelf.

"No thank you, just coffee." She filled her Styrofoam cup two-thirds of the way to allow for cream and sugar. As she ripped the top from a packet of sugar, Carl moved to fill his coffee cup.

Standing in the line to pay, Carl refused the five dollar bill she offered. "I said this one's on me." As he dug in his pocket, extracting a twenty, he asked, "So, how were your first couple of days?"

"I'm ready for something a little more taxing than reading." She smiled.

His knowing laugh eased a little of her tension. "I'm sorry, but I couldn't help the trip. When the big guy says jump, you just ask how high."

As they took a seat at a table close to the front of the cafeteria, Lacy wondered whether a double meaning existed in the man's words, or was Carl simply making a joke?

"In fact, here comes the big guy now." Carl motioned over her shoulder.

To exhibit an air of confidence and professionalism Lacy kept her seat, fighting the urge to turn and look. Instead, she gathered her composure, eager to make a good first impression. This job meant everything to her and Jessie.

Beneath the table, her palms began to sweat. Nonchalantly, she uncurled her fingers, wiped them on her skirt, and prayed that when she shook the VP's hand hers wouldn't be clammy.

Lacy waited until he stood at the head of the table before she raised her gaze slowly, confidently.

The room began to spin, the floor tilted. She tried to inhale a breath, but there was no air left in the room. She almost gasped, feeling like a fish out of water. She'd never fainted, yet when she stared into Wyatt's dusky blue eyes she wanted to do just that. From the corner of her eye Lacy saw Carl's mouth move, but she couldn't hear a word. Her head had filled with a gauzy substance, muffling sound and intelligent thought.

When Wyatt extended his hand she robotically pushed her chair away from the table, rose and accepted it. Warm and inviting, memories flooded her mind and body at his touch. It had been only five days ago that the strong fingers cradling her hand had caressed every part of her body.

"...David Anderson. DW we call him," concluded Carl.

Lacy's heart raced. She fought to grasp onto something tangible to reel herself back into the game. No matter what happened this past week, the man standing before her with an expressionless mask on his face could make or break her career. She gulped a breath of air and gathered what was left of her aplomb.

Lacy forced a smile that made her face feel like it was cracking as Wyatt released her hand. "DW? Mmm…let me guess, David Wyatt Anderson."

Carl beamed. "See? I told you she was sharp. Our girl has been doing her homework."

Lacy didn't care for the skeptical look on Wyatt's face.

"Yes, I can see that. Lariat, did you say? Welcome to Dunbar Semiconductors. We're happy to have you on our team." His response lacked enthusiasm.

Oh my God, surely he didn't think last weekend had anything to do with her position here? He couldn't possibly believe that she'd set him up.

Lacy felt like she was balancing on a tightrope. If she moved either way she'd fall. Everything she knew about Wyatt was wrong. He wasn't a good-for-nothing cowboy. The trendy gray suit he wore said he was a successful businessman, her *boss's* boss.

So, where did that leave them?

She froze. Wyatt and Carl had just spent the last couple of days together. She remembered the way Jay and his rodeo pals had talked about women. Had Wyatt confided in his friend about their relationship?

Lacy's stomach did a triple somersault and then biffed the landing, making her body sway.

Oh God, did Carl know they'd slept together? She searched Carl's face and saw nothing that indicated he knew something was afoot.

Lacy's dreams and plans seemed to vanish in a plume of smoke. What was she going to do? She couldn't work for Wyatt and continue to sleep with him.

Her gaze scanned his perfect form. And there was no way she could see him every day and not think about how he felt moving inside her. How her body craved his. Even now her nipples tightened, ached, but were thankfully hidden beneath her blazer. A creamy wetness pooled at the apex of her thighs.

"You have time to join us?" Carl asked.

Wyatt glanced at the large black and white clock hanging on the west wall. "I have a meeting in fifteen minutes." He turned back and looked at Lacy. "But Lariat, why don't you stop by my office around eleven? We'll have a little chat, if that's okay with your boss." His voice was so calm it sent a tremor through Lacy.

Carl smiled, his eyes twinkling with something Lacy refused to try to read. "Sure. I'm giving her a tour of the lab as soon as we finish our coffee. Eleven will be fine."

Lacy took her seat as Wyatt proceeded to head to the coffee dispenser.

Appreciation glowed on Carl's face. "Wow. You made quite an impression on DW."

Oh yeah, quite an impression. She had spread her legs for Carl's boss on the first night they met. She knew the deep, satisfying moans of passion his boss made when he reached climax. The feel of his thick cock buried deep inside her pussy — even the taste of him upon her tongue. Hell, she could even tell Carl the length of his boss's cock.

Lacy fought to hold back her tears. She didn't know whether to be angry with Wyatt or mad at herself. It was obvious that he wasn't *just* a cowboy.

Well she was paying for her snap judgment and prejudices. Asking a few simple questions could've curtailed this unfortunate episode. What would happen next was anyone's guess.

Wyatt jerked back his hand as coffee surged over his cup. To say he was stunned to see Lacy at the table with Carl would be mild. He'd been caught somewhere between elation and foreboding. Wyatt shook his hand and silently cursed. The spot between his thumb and index finger was turning red. He reached for his cup, tipping it gently so he wouldn't spill any more.

This incident simply brought home how little he knew about the woman.

Had she known who he was all along?

Surely not.

With Lacy it was what you see is what you get — unless she was a brilliant actress. Nah, she couldn't fake what had happened between them.

Still, Wyatt wasn't prepared for the complications this created at Dunbar Semiconductors and in his professional life. He had served as a role model within the department to keep personal and business relationships separate. What was he going to do now? There was no way he could work with Lacy and not want to climb in her panties every minute of the day. She was like a drug he just had to have.

Wyatt paid for his coffee. As he passed by Lacy's table he nodded to Carl, his gaze gravitating to her. "I'll see you at eleven." He sipped his coffee quickly to hide the smile that tried to emerge.

A shadow passed across her eyes. "Yes, eleven."

The walk to the conference room in the next building gave Wyatt time to gather his thoughts. This was indeed a dilemma. Bottom line, they were lovers. She couldn't continue to work beneath him.

Beneath him?

As he sat down at the mahogany table, Wyatt was glad that no one could see where his mind was, because it stood hard and at attention between his thighs. Someone had thought ahead when they designed this table. A long skirt of wood before his knees allowed no more than his feet to show to those on the other side of the table.

Just the thought of his cock thrusting into Lacy's liquid heat shifted his libido into high gear. His pulse and breathing increased. His erection pressed against the zipper of his gray dress slacks. It had been days since he'd tasted the sweet nectar between her thighs, and he was ready to sample her again.

How was he to manage a department, knowing she sat within thirty feet of his office?

As the first presenter approached the Proxima—the electronic overhead run by the computer attached to it—he was already slipping into a fantasy. The dim lights did nothing more than set the mood.

The first thing Wyatt would do when he was alone with Lacy was release her hair. The severe knot she had it twisted into made her eyes slant, it was so tight. Then he'd run his fingers through the silky strands. He cupped himself, trying to ease the ache in his swollen cock.

Next to go would be that thick blazer that hid her breasts from his eyes. The shirt and bra wouldn't last long either. But what excited him the most would be stripping her of her skirt and panties, touching the pink swollen flesh between her thighs and sucking her clit until she writhed and screamed in ecstasy.

Now that's exactly what he planned to do in...he glanced down at his watch...about nine hours, fifteen minutes and twenty seconds, after he got her home.

From eight to ten-thirty Wyatt listened to one presentation after another. What the three presenters said about the proposed sensor went in one ear and out the other.

"Hey, Charlie, I'd like to review some of your slides in more detail. Can you email me a copy of the presentations?" Charlie flashed Wyatt a grin and nodded. He'd review the material later, just in case someone referred to the meeting.

Now he just had to make it through the next thirty minutes before facing Lacy.

Lacy moved around three large brown metal containers, following in Carl's wake. She had on her regulation lab coat, an ESD — electrostatic discharge band — and a pair of safety glasses that she thought looked like a really ugly set of goggles.

"The Sandric program has three testers. Each tester has two separate handlers." Carl moved around the bulky machines pointing to trays that a technician in a matching lab coat was slipping plastic reels into. Each reel held one hundred minute chips, or sensors.

The young technician smiled. His hand slipped and the reel hit the floor scattering chips everywhere. Lacy gasped at the amount of money lying at her feet. She carefully stepped backwards.

Frantically, the man dropped to his knees. His gaze shot to her, then Carl as he began to pick up the little black and gray chips. "Carl, I'm sorry, I—"

"It's okay, Matt. These things happen. Be more careful in the future." The wrinkles in Carl's forehead expressed his displeasure, but at least he'd handled the technician's clumsiness in a professional manner. Lacy had to appreciate that.

Carl's voice interrupted her thoughts. "Lariat has a meeting with DW."

Lariat. Sooner or later Wyatt would slip and call her Lacy. She might as well start padding the way. "Please, Carl, call me Lacy."

"Nickname?"

She nodded.

"Lacy it is. I've got a few more things in the lab to take care of." He gave her a mischievous smile that deepened the laugh lines in the corners of his mouth. "Think you can find your way back upstairs?"

Could she? Did she want to? Thoughts of meeting with Wyatt twisted her stomach and caused beads of perspiration to gather above her upper lip as she tossed her lab jacket and goggles in a bin.

"I think I can manage. But if you don't see me for the next couple of days, send out a search party."

"You got it." Carl bent to help Matt retrieve the scattered chips from the floor.

Lacy took the stairs instead of the elevator to prolong the time it took to get to Wyatt's office. Unfortunately, the stairs ended right outside his assistant's door.

Hesitating, Lacy squared her shoulders, took a deep cleansing breath and walked in. Crystal was absent from her desk. She released a heavy sigh of relief and was just about to turn and leave when Wyatt stepped out of his office.

"Lacy."

"Wyatt."

For a moment they stood there staring at each other in silence. She didn't know if that was a good sign or not.

"Come on in." He held open the door. As she walked past him, the tip of her nipple accidentally brushed his arm, sending electrical shock waves through her breast. She barely held back the moan lingering in her throat.

Walking into his plush office, the scent of lemon furniture polish teased her nose. She'd noticed that all the upper management offices were done in mahogany. It must be the wood of choice in the upper echelons of the business world.

Moving down the chain of command, tables and desks were of oak and softer woods, and in some cases metal. For example, her desk looked like nothing more than pressed wood held together by gray metal.

When the door shut behind Lacy a chill raced up her spine. She turned and landed right into his arms. Before she could take a breath his mouth melded to hers.

Lacy knew she should step away, break the kiss, but her traitorous legs refused to move. The gentleness of his lips against hers as his tongue probed, asking—not demanding—entrance, made her open to him. Her arms rose to encircle his neck. His hands moved slowly along her back, grasping her ass and pressing her hips to his. He was hard, ready for her. And she was wet and eager to taste more of him.

Then reality hit. This couldn't be happening, legally, ethically and morally. They were colleagues now. There was no room in their lives to be lovers.

Lacy was the first to pull away. "Wyatt, we can't do this."

"Why?" He refused to relinquish her. Instead he ground his hips against hers. "I missed you." He kissed the soft spot behind her ear that made her tremble.

"I need this job." Her sensitive nipples rasped against the cloth restraining them. She wanted to moan from the discomfort. But more than that, she wanted to tear her clothes off and spread herself on his conference table screaming, "Take me, I'm yours". Instead, she attempted to step away, but Wyatt's arms tightened around her.

"I know." He buried his face into her shoulder. "But I need you."

God, if only that were true. If only there was a future for them.

"How's Jessie?" he whispered into her ear, a hand floating down to stroke her thigh.

Did he really want to know? "She's doing well. I can't wait to see her tonight."

Wyatt released her and then went to his computer. "When are you leaving?" His fingers tapped the keyboard.

What was he doing? "Five." Lacy inched a little closer and realized that he was looking at a calendar.

"Can you make it five-thirty, so I can go with you?"

Her jaw dropped. "Really?" Surprise lingered in that one word. Then she began to shake her head. "No, no, this is all wrong. Wyatt, I have to think about what's best for Jessie. This job provides me a decent opportunity to support her. Get us out of the dump we're living in. You— me, we can't be an *us*." Breathless, she whispered, "I can't sleep with you anymore."

Soft blue eyes turned cold. A nerve twitched in his jaw as he strode around the desk.

She stumbled backwards.

He reached for her and she dodged his grasp. "That's unacceptable. I'll find you another job."

"I don't need your help." Her tone was a little more defensive than she had planned.

How could she explain to him that she couldn't trust anyone, including him, not when her job was on the line. She hated this whole awkward situation. They didn't know each other. She couldn't change her entire path in life based on one hot weekend with a mysterious cowboy.

And Wyatt had sure looked the part last weekend. Although she had to admit he looked mighty fine in dress clothes. She shook the lust from her feeble mind.

Lacy needed to succeed on her own. She needed this job, the money it offered, the security, the medical benefits. She needed it all for Jessie.

Just because Wyatt didn't exactly fit the stereotype of a worthless cowboy didn't mean she could throw away all she'd worked toward. Her experience with men up to this point left much to be desired. She had to protect herself.

"We'll have to think of something, because I'm not letting you go." He made another dive for her, catching her forearm.

She yanked her arm, unsuccessfully, as his fingers tightened. "You don't have a choice."

Like an arrogant man, he said, "I do too. I'm the boss."

When he played that card, Lacy's breath left her lungs in a sudden gush. "Boss? In this work environment only. My personal life is my own. I won't allow you to jeopardize my future here, even if I have to go to personnel."

Checkmate! Your turn…

His hands jerked away from her. A heated expression that could have ignited a forest fire took over his face. She almost expected to see steam emerge from his ears. When his nostrils flared, she wondered if the card she'd played was worth the fury in his eyes.

He squared his shoulders. "Thank you, Miss Mason. I don't believe we have *anything* else to discuss." He turned his back on her, walked behind his imposing desk and took a seat in the leather chair. As if she had already left the room, he began to press heavy fingers to the keyboard of his computer.

Lacy was trembling. It was as if he'd shut a door, she stood on one side, he on the other. This wasn't the way she'd wanted it to end. She'd wanted it to end with her in his arms. His cock buried deep inside pussy. She wanted to feel his warm, wet mouth on her breasts, his fingers dancing across her skin. She wanted forever with this man. Yet that was never going to happen. A deep sorrow weighted her shoulders. If only there was something she could say or do to change the situation. But she knew it had to end here—now. She had to think about Jessie and their future.

For a brief moment she remained frozen in place. Wyatt slowly raised his head. He pinned her with a steely glare. "Is there anything else, Miss Mason?" The coolness in his tone sent a shiver up her spine. Her tongue moistened her lips.

"No, Mr. Anderson, I believe that we are *through.*" The finality in the last word almost crushed her.

Lacy's composure held until she walked out Wyatt's door. Emotion burned her eyes. Choking back unshed tears, she promised herself she wouldn't cry, not here. As she turned to walk away, she bumped into Carl.

His eyes narrowed. "Lacy, are you okay? Did something happen?" He glanced toward Wyatt's office.

She forced a weak smile. "No, I'm just a little overwhelmed. This job is important to me."

He started to place a hand on her shoulder and then withdrew sharply. "Well, don't worry. After this week it'll be old hat to you."

She glanced in the direction of Wyatt's office.

"Relax, everyone has a learning curve. Come on, it's lunchtime and I'm buying."

"Oh, I can't. I mean, I'd love to join you but we'll go Dutch." How could she turn her boss down? Networking was the key to success. Yet going out for lunch each day would be a killer on her budget.

"I won't hear of it." Carl wagged his brows. "Besides, the company's paying for it."

She forced a chuckle from her lips. "Well, if that's the case, sure."

"Great. Meet me out in the parking lot in about ten minutes." Carl turned and hurried through Wyatt's open door.

Breathe, Lacy. Everything will be okay. But how could a mess like this have a happy ending?

Chapter Thirteen

ဢ

Wyatt was late. Impatiently, he waited his turn to walk through the rotating glass doors. He hated being late. It wasn't the appearance he wanted his staff to have of him.

Finally, it was his turn and he took the shuffling steps required to inch along at a snail's pace. When the glass doors released him, he hastened his stride, faltering when he saw who was in the car with Carl and John.

Carl had just purchased a brand new Jeep Cherokee that he was eager to show off. Lacy sat in the back, leaving the only place to sit right next to her. He started to ask Carl if he wanted to take his truck, then thought better of it. No way did he want to show any discord between Lacy and him.

Wyatt quietly folded himself into the backseat. Lacy scooted subtly toward the far door and away from him.

"How wonderful, Miss Mason is joining us." This was a little unorthodox. His staff had never invited a newbie to lunch with them. Especially when it was a working lunch. He'd have a talk with both of them when they returned.

Lacy faced him, her heavy lashes fluttering as she smiled. "Thank you, I appreciate the invitation."

Well done, thought Wyatt.

"Lacy." Carl glanced over his shoulder. "She goes by Lacy."

"Does she now? Well, Lacy, do you live around here?"

She squirmed in her seat. "No, I live in Gilbert."

Wyatt spread his knees apart, so that he touched her bare leg. She flashed him a look of disdain, but didn't attempt to move away. Instead, she gave her knee a little bounce that rubbed her silky skin against his pants. Then she flashed him a heated look.

He hadn't expected her reaction. His libido kicked in, did a somersault, and expected the next touch to be more intimate. Well, the old boy was going to be disappointed, because nothing more was going to happen, not here.

"A growing community." Wyatt wanted to do much more to Lacy then irritate her through a slight touch. He wanted to shake some sense into her. What they had together wasn't something to just toss aside.

But there was more to think about than lust. Jessie, their futures and careers.

"Isn't that where the rodeo was this weekend?" asked John. "By the way, how did you do?"

"DW rides in the rodeos. The ones that are close by," added Carl.

"He does?" Her eyes widened as she feigned surprise and interest. "How wonderful. Yes, how did you do?"

"Second in steer wrestling. In bareback, my rides were rather rough this weekend. Guess you could say I got screwed." Wyatt fixed his gaze to hers.

Lacy's jaw clenched. She licked her lips. "Easy to do when you're riding a stubborn *horse*." The wilting tone of her voice said she wanted to use the word "ass" instead.

John twisted in his seat. "Hey, you two are almost neighbors. DW lives in Chandler."

Well this was great chitchat, but they had business to discuss. "Carl, what's going on with Syborg in Toulouse?" Wyatt asked. "Does it look like it's going to cost us?"

"Tom's making arrangements to hop a plane tonight. You should have his travel authorization by three today. We think that Syborg is stressing the limits of the sensor when they weld it onto their board, possibly damaging the leads. Tom wants to review their procedure to determine if it's their problem or ours."

"If the issue is ours what's the plan of action?"

The business strategy continued until they pulled into a strip mall.

Lunch at Shangri-La, a Chinese restaurant on Alma School and Elliot, went better than expected. Hell, Lacy even made some recommendations for testing the stress levels of the sensor they were discussing.

She was an intelligent woman and if it wasn't for him wanting her so bad that his teeth hurt, she'd be a wonderful asset to Dunbar Semiconductors.

When they pulled into Dunbar's parking lot, Lacy scrambled from the Jeep. Then she wedged herself between Carl and John, neither one having a problem with her close proximity, except for Wyatt. He didn't like the smiles she gave them or the ones she received in return. Her light, tinkling laughter made his skin heat.

"Carl and John, let's meet for a couple minutes. Wrap this thing up." Both men hung back as Wyatt addressed them.

"I'll see you later." Lacy tossed a wave in their direction.

"Later, Lacy," both men said in unison. Their sappy gazes followed her as she swiped her badge and entered the rotating glass doors.

Then Carl turned to him. "What do you think, DW? She's something, isn't she? I think her suggestion on tap sensitivity just might work."

"She shows promise. But, let's not lose sight. Lacy is a newbie, and after meeting her...well, let's just say that the sexual harassment classes everyone took should be taken to heart. I don't think I need to elaborate?"

The small shakes of each man's head confirmed that nothing more needed to be said. Now if only he could follow his own advice.

Back-to-back meetings kept Wyatt preoccupied until five-thirty. He flicked the light off in his office and locked his door.

Lacy was surely gone, but he couldn't resist swinging by her desk. When he entered her cubicle he pulled to an abrupt halt. Her shoulders were bent over her desk as she frantically wrote something on a sheet of paper.

"Why are you still here?" He hadn't anticipated the boom in his voice, or the shriek of surprise that came from her lips as she sat upright.

"I'm finishing up my notes on the tap sensitivity concept." She frowned, leaning forward, her forearm sliding over her paper.

"It probably won't work, Lacy." When her eyes narrowed, Wyatt felt like the stuff scraped off the bottom of a shoe. He had never before dissuaded anyone from experimenting and reaching for solutions. That was what research and development was all about. Still, he had lashed out and belittled Lacy's idea.

"Wyatt, you're not going to give me a chance, are you?" The hurt in her eyes, on her face, was humbling.

"Lacy—"

She rose so quickly that she stumbled, almost falling into his arms. He took a quick step back as she swung around, crumpling her proposal in a tight fist and then cramming the sheet of papers against his chest, hard.

"Fine, I'm out of here." She didn't even stop to turn her lights off. Her hands trembled as she grabbed the strap of her purse. The leather bag swung around, striking him in the thigh as her shoulder whacked his arm none to gently.

He thought to reach out to her, to apologize for his lack of support, but pride held him motionless. This was his territory. Slowly, he raised her crumpled plans in front of him and studied her proposal.

He nodded, liking what he saw. Lacy was right on top of the problem. She was good, damn good. Her idea on testing tap-sensitivity just might work.

A spot of wax almost sent Lacy tumbling to the floor as her foot skidded across the linoleum with a squeak, leaving a black mark. She faltered, throwing herself against the wall for support.

Shit. She leaned against the cool wall, tears of frustration burning her eyes.

The ragged breath she released helped to calm the storm of emotion brewing inside her. The tendons in her throat tightened as she swallowed hard. With a hefty shove, she pushed away from the wall and began to hurry down the hall.

A maintenance man turned the corner just as she did. She attempted to return the smile the elderly gentleman offered, but she knew it fell short. Everything she had worked for, had dreamed of, was slipping through her fingers—all because she had let her guard down and eased the ache between her thighs.

Her steps quickened in anger. Her fists swung by her sides. Would she continue to make one mistake after another? Was she destined to always choose the wrong man?

God, she was stupid.

As Lacy entered the spinning glass door it sped up, giving her a firm whack on the ass, pushing her forward and out as if she was being physically tossed out of Dunbar Semiconductors. Lacy pitched forward releasing an exasperated breath as she gained her footing and tugged down her rising skirt. What more could happen?

She didn't have to wait long to find out. As she climbed into her car and jammed the key in the ignition, she saw Wyatt exiting the revolving doors. Quickly, she twisted the metal between her fingers. *Click. Click.*

Her palm landed hard on the steering wheel. "Start, damn you."

From the corner of her eye she could see Wyatt approaching, and he was smiling. In a fit of irritation, she rolled the key over again, a little too hard as the metal started to bend. *Click. Click.*

This just couldn't be happening.

The light tapping on her window drew her head up sharply. The grin was gone from his face, but he couldn't hide the bright gleam in his eyes.

"Need some help?" Before she could reach the lock, he opened the door wide.

Irritation crawled across her skin. "No." She leaned out and pulled on the door handle, but his grip and the fact that he stepped in front of the door kept it open.

"Lacy—"

"I don't need your help," she enunciated each word firmly, even though she knew that without his assistance she would have to call a taxi. She couldn't afford a trip to the hospital to see Jessie, one back to her apartment and then to work tomorrow morning. That was only if the mechanics could *fix* her car, and where was she going to find the money to pay for the repairs and tow truck?

Still, she wasn't going to let Wyatt know she needed him.

"Get out," he said, a thin edge of a growl to his voice.

"Fuck you." She snapped her head forward. Wrong thing to say. Wrong move to make.

Lacy didn't see Wyatt lunge forward, but she felt his strong fingers wrap around her biceps and jerk with a force that propelled her from the car. She released a gasp of surprise as she landed hard against his chest. Before she could push away, he wrapped his arms around her.

Her eyes widened as she glanced around for onlookers. The last thing she needed was to be caught in an awkward situation with the boss.

"Be still and listen," his voice dropped dangerously low, "because I'm only going to say this once." The rapid beat of his heart matched hers as she breathed in his scent, a spicy fresh smell that wrapped around her as tightly as his arms. She felt his rapid pulse through his fingertips. The glow in his eyes had morphed into something darker. "You will get your purse and walk calmly over to my truck and climb in. And you'll do it without a word." She attempted to wiggle free, but his grip tightened, burying her nose deeper into his masculine heat. "I'll take you to see Jessie, then to dinner, and then back to my place where I plan to *fuck you* all night long."

Lacy stilled. The thought of having this man between her thighs, deep inside, left her speechless, not to mention aroused. Unconsciously, her body softened, melting into his. Hands that had been wedged against his broad chest, stroked a path down his sides, then around his waist, her fingers fisting into his shirt. Electricity stung her nipples.

They tingled, beading, sending a live current straight to her belly. Desire dampened her panties. She wanted this man with a vengeance.

Lacy managed to find her voice. "We can't." Regret was something she had learned to live with. This wasn't going to work, him—her. She knew it. He knew it.

"We can and we will." He released her, but not before he planted a kiss atop her head. "Now get your purse, lock the doors and come on—I'm hungry."

Lacy scrambled into the car, knowing that Wyatt had a clear view of her thigh as her skirt hiked up. His groan confirmed it, and she paused.

Was she going to let this man take control? A heavy sigh eased from her lips. What would it feel like for someone else to make decisions, to be responsible? Jay had never taken care of anything. Hell, he was still running from responsibility and commitment.

She was tired of being alone, tired of balancing on the edge of a cliff with no one to catch her should she fall.

Jessie left no room for failure. Each day was a trial, a test of Lacy's courage. Sometimes she felt like letting go, giving up. But one look into her daughter's innocent eyes and she knew she had to fight for their future, fight for Jessie's life.

As she wiggled out of the car, she heard someone call out, "Car trouble?"

Great. Lacy straightened, tugging on the hem of her skirt as loose gravel popped beneath Carl's feet. Wyatt flashed her an uneasy look, and then took several steps back, putting distance between them. Lacy knew she shouldn't let his reaction affect her, but it did. Wyatt didn't want anyone to know about their affair.

This wasn't fucking la-la land. There wasn't a relationship building between the two of them, only a dirty little secret to be hidden.

"Won't start," Wyatt mumbled.

"Battery?" Carl moved around to the front of the car. "Pop the hood. Let's have a look."

Lacy reached beneath the steering wheel and gave the lever a pull. The catch gave and the hood squeaked as Carl raised it.

Wyatt joined Carl as he began to tug on the battery cables. "Maybe she needs a jump."

"Could be the alternator," Wyatt offered.

Quietly, Lacy prayed for a dead battery. A battery cost thirty, forty dollars? The alternator was a much more expensive problem. And once a mechanic got beneath the hood, no telling what he'd find. If only she could trash this piece of crap.

"I've got a set of jumper cables." Carl smiled. "Don't worry, Lacy. We'll have your car running in no time."

She stood quietly beside Wyatt. Without making eye contact, he whispered, "You're still going home with me tonight."

"No." Her voice was soft, breathless.

"We'll see." There was something in his tone that sent a shiver up Lacy's spine. She had no idea why Wyatt was being so stubborn. The man was totally unreasonable, and she planned to tell him so the first chance she got.

Within minutes her Ford Escort was humming. It was more of a cough, but it was running. Carl slammed the hood shut. "Something's draining the battery. Can't promise it'll start up tomorrow morning." He reached into his pocket and extracted his business card and a pen, and began to scribble something on it. "Here's my home telephone number. Call me if you need a ride."

Lacy accepted the card. She couldn't risk having no transportation. "Do you think the Ford dealership on Mesa Drive is still open?"

Carl glanced at his watch. "Should be. You want me to follow you and then take you home?"

Wyatt stepped forward, his body rigid. "It's on my way. Why don't I follow her and take her home?"

"Actually, I believe the dealership offers a ride service. You both have done so much already. Thank you." She slipped behind the wheel, waved and punched the car into reverse, but not before she saw the expression on Wyatt's face. He wasn't happy.

In her rearview mirror she watched the two men talk and then separate, heading for their vehicles.

Lacy pressed firmly on the accelerator and prayed the car didn't die before she reached the dealership.

Wyatt watched Lacy speak with the Service Advisor standing beside her car. She was frowning and the man was making wide gestures with his hands. Wyatt worried that the man would take advantage of her, so he exited his truck and approached.

The serviceman was all grins and smiles until Wyatt slipped his arm around Lacy's shoulders. She startled, but didn't pull away.

He gave her a little squeeze. "Honey, I'll pick the car up tomorrow." Lacy's mouth gaped open.

The man's face dropped. "Uh, Mr. Mason."

Wyatt jutted out his right hand. "Yes." A flicker of surprise flashed across Lacy's face as the serviceman clutched his hand and shook.

"Is it the battery?" Wyatt asked.

"Well, we won't know until we get under the hood."

The scornful expression on Lacy's face told Wyatt that she hadn't gotten the same answer.

"Did you give my wife a card, so I can call you tomorrow regarding the repairs?"

The man fumbled in his shirt pocket and extracted his business card handing it to Wyatt. Wyatt didn't miss the look of shock that filtered across Lacy's face as he placed the man's card into his shirt pocket. Nor did she contradict him. Evidently she was too tired to argue when he started to lead her away.

"Thank you, Mr. Gould. C'mon, baby, let's go home."

Wyatt opened his truck door and Lacy slid in. He followed, liking how it felt to have her sitting next to him as he started the engine and put the vehicle into gear.

They had traveled two miles and neither said a word. She was quiet, too quiet, and he wondered how bad it would be when she released the wrath of Lacy upon him.

When she finally spoke, she was eerily calm. "This isn't going to work, Wyatt."

He looked straight ahead into traffic. "It'll work. We'll *make* it work." He glanced sideways at her.

Shaking her head, an uneasy laugh squeezed from her lips. The color had drained from her face. She looked weary. "Dunbar won't allow it to work. You'll ruin your career and mine will be finished before it even begins." She swallowed hard. "Wyatt, I need this job." It was almost a plea.

Deep down, he knew she was right. But he wasn't ready to let her go.

Nothing more was said for the remainder of the trip to the hospital. Jessie was asleep as they entered her room. She looked so small and helpless in the big bed that dwarfed her.

The love in Lacy's eyes as she stroked her daughter's hair put Wyatt to shame. All he could think about was his libido as Lacy fought to save her daughter's life and planned for their future.

Lacy was an amazing woman. She didn't ask for anything for herself. Every step, every move she made was toward a better life for her daughter. She was the most unselfish woman he had ever met. She was special.

The evening nurse approached. She hugged Lacy. "Hon, she probably won't wake up for the remainder of the night. Our little girl didn't have a very good day today." The woman whispered, "I just learned that the number two person on the list died. It was sudden."

Lacy's head bobbed. Worry creased her brow. Jessie had been moved up the donor recipient list. And by the little girl's appearance tonight, her health was rapidly failing.

The nurse checked Jessie's IV and then turned to Lacy. "Go home and get some sleep."

Indecision rippled across Lacy's face.

Wyatt reached for her. Again, she didn't pull away as he embraced her. She was cold to the touch. When she looked up at him, she did so with haunted eyes.

The tiny hairs on his arms rose. "C'mon, baby."

She drifted from his embrace and stood over Jessie, and he followed. Lacy's chest rose and fell with emotion as she leaned forward and kissed Jessie's pale cheek. Her lips moved, but no words emerged. Wyatt could barely make out her mouthing, "I love you," before she turned and stepped into his arms.

For a moment he simply held her. Then he led her out of Jessie's room, out of the hospital and into his truck. As he climbed in she scooted to his side. He swung his arm around her pulling her tight to him. She fit perfectly against the curve of his body.

Wyatt pulled onto the I-10 ramp and entered the freeway. "Hungry?" Traffic had thinned and he was thankful he wouldn't have to fight his way back to the east valley.

"No, but you are. Stop wherever you want." Her tone was listless, empty.

"How about we stop by your place, you pick up your clothes for tomorrow and I take you to my house." A car darted in front of Wyatt and he laid on the horn.

"Whatever." Her response held no enthusiasm.

Now that wasn't good. She wasn't even going to argue with him. "Honey, Jessie's like her mom—hard as steel. She's going to be okay."

Lacy gazed up at him and forced a smile that didn't make it to her eyes. She nodded. "Thank you."

He hugged her closer, kissed her forehead. "For what?"

She didn't answer and he didn't ask again.

A wrought iron sign arched high above the entrance that identified Wyatt's home as the Busting A Ranch. As he pulled into his driveway, the truck's bright headlights beamed across his Spanish-style home as if he was presenting it to Lacy via spotlight.

She straightened in the seat. "You live here?"

He wondered what it looked like through her eyes. He had forty-five acres, mostly planted in alfalfa, a four-thousand-square-foot house, a barn and stables for his livestock. He even had a lighted roping arena, a swimming pool and a Jacuzzi. Compared to her apartment, it must look like a mansion.

"I grew up here." He pulled the truck to a stop. "Still has the old swing in the backyard that I broke my arm flying out of." He laughed, remembering the fear on his mother's face as he'd walked into the kitchen, his arm twisted into an unnatural angle.

Lacy leaned forward, taking in the scenery. "It's beautiful, Wyatt."

Pride swelled his chest. He didn't know why it meant so much to him that she like his home, but it did.

He climbed out of the vehicle and held the door for her. He helped her down from the truck, grabbed her bag with one arm, draped the other around her shoulders and headed toward the house.

"Don't you need to feed your animals?"

Wyatt inserted his key and opened the front door. "I called ahead and had a neighbor take care of it."

As Lacy stepped inside she audibly sucked in her breath. The décor was western. It had a rugged beauty from the heavy leather and wood furniture to the wrought iron chandelier. The Mexican tile on the floor was broken up by tiny horseshoes embedded sporadically throughout. A massive flagstone fireplace made her feel insignificant in comparison.

A wealth of family history was spread throughout the room in the form of pictures and rodeo memorabilia.

Wyatt tossed his keys on a coffee table and immediately reached for her, spinning her around to face him. She couldn't read the expression on his face, but his dusky blue eyes had darkened to an even deeper blue.

He pulled her to him. "Do you like it?" His lips were a breath away from hers.

Her tongue moistened her bottom lip. "Wyatt, it's gorgeous."

Their mouths came together in a gentle exploration as he stroked her, caressed her mouth and worshipped her lips. His arms held her close to the warmth of his body. He was hard, his erection burning into her stomach.

Lacy didn't know if she could give him what he wanted or needed tonight. So many things had happened today. But nothing pulled the rug out from under her feet like the news of Jessie's deterioration. It was a constant reminder of how brittle the future was. She couldn't live without Jessie. She didn't want to.

Wyatt's strong fingers weaved through hers. "C'mon, I'll show you where you can put your things."

He led her down a hall and opened the first door they came to. He stepped aside, releasing her hand as she entered what could only be the master bedroom, *his* bedroom. Impressive was putting it mildly. In fact, it was bigger than her entire apartment.

Wyatt tossed her bag on the four-poster king-size bed. Then he strolled over to the fireplace. Where the fireplace in the living room was flagstone, this was slate. Burnished autumn colors spread across the floor and traveled up the fireplace.

Extracting a long match from a brass holder, he struck it against the stone. The pungent, tart scent of sulfur arose as he tucked the match into the wood stacked neatly within the grate. The tinder ignited and the scent of fresh pine chased away the sulfurous odor.

Hand on the mantel, Wyatt stared into the hearth, watching the fire breathe and take on life as the wood crackled and popped. His shoulders rose and fell heavily.

Slowly, he turned to face her. She watched the play of emotions flicker across his face. "I realize you've had a hell of a day, but will you stay with me, here, tonight?"

Chapter Fourteen

ॐ

Wyatt's arms closed gently around Lacy. "Wyatt?" Lacy murmured against his broad chest. She inhaled the light scent of starch off his crisp shirt.

He pressed a finger to her parted lips. "*Shhh*, you don't have to do or say anything, Lacy. Just let me take care of you tonight."

It wasn't necessarily what he said, but how he said it. There was a softness, a *caring* in his low voice that warmed her blood and made her feel so right in his embrace.

For a moment, he simply held her, shared his strength, his support. It flowed through her veins like honey, tender and sweet.

Unshed tears blossomed in her eyes. He was everything she had dreamed of in a man. Strong and rooted. He knew what he wanted in life. His job, his home, the way he managed the people at Dunbar, all spoke of pride and stability. He was sensitive and caring. From the beginning, when she needed him, when things with Jessie were teetering, he was there by her side. A stranger had become her rock, her strength.

Someday he would make a wonderful father and husband to a lucky woman. The thought caused a rogue tear to fall.

He held her at arms length with one hand and wiped the tear from her cheek with the other. "C'mon."

Wyatt led Lacy into the adjoining bathroom and she couldn't help the gasp that squeezed from her lips. The bathroom alone was as big as her bedroom. There was a huge shower surrounded by glass blocks, two vanity areas with dual sinks and a Jacuzzi tub to die for.

He released her long enough to turn the knobs of the tub. Water splashed against the porcelain surface as he leaned over and tested the temperature. When he was satisfied, he reached for an hourglass-shaped bottle sitting on the bathtub's marble counter and poured a little of its contents into the now-swirling water, making the heady scent of cinnamon rise hot and spicy in the air. Then he turned to face Lacy, his eyes so dark and sensual that her breath caught.

Without a word, he crooked his index finger, beckoning her to his side. Her feet took over and answered his call, coming to a stop before him. Slowly he began to undress her.

His hands were gentle as he touched her skin, stroking the fine hairs on her arms. Her nerve endings tingled as he brushed her shirt off her shoulders, allowing the silk to drop to the floor.

"So soft," he murmured, reaching for her.

Blue eyes held hers as his deft fingers released the clasp of her bra. The hooks sprang loose, but it was Wyatt who unveiled her breasts. His heated gaze caressed her flesh as he tossed the scrap of lace atop her shirt.

"Beautiful," he hummed.

As if choreographed, their breathing became heavy, moving as one.

He worked quickly, releasing the button and zipper of her skirt, revealing her lace bikini panties along with her thigh-high stockings. Then he stepped back and stared at her. "Every time I look at you I'm bewitched." His voice was hoarse, igniting the flames of her desire.

Her breasts felt heavy. Her nipples tingled. Spasmodic tremors tightened her pussy. The need to feel him deep inside her built like a raging fire.

Weaving slightly, she stepped from the skirt pooling at her ankles. Using one foot and then the other, she disposed of her heels, kicking them out of the way.

Strong hands closed around her biceps as he turned and backed her toward the marble edge of the Jacuzzi. She felt the cool stone against her thighs as she sat. Wyatt quickly turned the water off and pressed the button that started the jets humming, churning the water and further raising the scent of cinnamon into the air.

When he faced her, naked male hunger stared out at her. "I need to fuck you, but not yet."

Another flood of desire dampened her thighs. He stepped forward, knelt and proceeded to strip her of her remaining clothing.

His palms were hot as they caressed her thigh, rolling the stocking down her leg. As the silk slipped off her foot, he massaged gently and then pressed a kiss to her big toe, sparking a smile from her lips. After he repeated the same thing with her other foot, he stood, pulling her toward him so their bodies were almost touching.

Eyes fixed to hers, he slipped his thumbs into the waistband of her panties. As he drew her underwear off her hips, he kissed the sensitive spot between her breasts. Slowly moving the lace down her thighs, his mouth followed, burning a path down her stomach. When at last her panties tangled around her ankles, Wyatt's mouth touched the apex of her thighs.

"Mmmm…" The growl came from somewhere deep in his throat.

Stepping out of her underwear, her thighs parted and he pressed his mouth to her flesh.

Lacy swayed. Boneless legs threatened to give out as his tongue stroked across her slit. She shuddered, placing her palms on his shoulders for support. His touch was light, teasing, not meant to satisfy, but to entice. Her pussy responded, releasing her juices for him to savor.

He inhaled deeply then moved away, leaving her longing. She reached for him but he shook his head, stepping beyond her hands.

Wyatt slowly divested himself of clothing, drawing out their anticipation. She was mesmerized by his hands as they worked to undo each button, displaying curly black chest hair a little at a time as his shirt fell open. She took a step forward and he matched it with one in the opposite direction.

She glared at his wooden expression. But the twinkle in his eyes was his downfall. The man was playing with her desire, baiting her with the need to feel his naked body against her own.

She frowned, surprised when her voice growled, "Dammit, Wyatt, take your clothes off and come here."

His chuckle was gravelly and short as he stripped down to his briefs and then remembered he still had shoes on. One hand held on to the countertop while his other one pulled at a shoe. The pants wadded around his ankles made it impossible to achieve what he wanted.

Lacy laughed. It felt good to laugh.

He hopped, nearly falling forward before resorting to using the toe of one foot to wedge the shoe off another. He finally stepped free of his pants.

Muscles rippled across his sun-bronzed chest. Tendons bulged in his tight biceps and arms as he finally stood only in his briefs. Her gaze followed the curly ebony hair of his chest down his taut stomach, to where it swirled around his bellybutton and disappeared beyond the snowy cotton.

The palms of her hands itched, her fingernails scraping across them trying to ease the longing burning within her.

"Forget the bath, I need you inside me." Her voice sounded thin and tight with passion.

He moved toward the tub, the humming of the jets dying before he turned to face her.

The tingling sensation rippling through her nipples was increasing to sharp prickles of excitement. A strong pulse throbbed between her thighs, begging for his cock to fill her. She needed to touch him and be touched in return.

When he tugged his briefs past his engorged erection, a groan emerged from somewhere deep in her throat. That little ardent sound was enough to make Wyatt hastily push his briefs all the way down. Kicking them across the room, he quickly took the several steps needed to press their heated bodies together.

The minute their flesh touched, Lacy released a sigh of unmitigated pleasure. Her skin breathed in his energy, his passion. She fed on his ardor, eager to taste his desire. He held her as if she was a fragile piece of glass.

"Touch me, Wyatt. Touch all of me." She hated the plea in her voice, but she needed to feel his hands upon her breasts, teasing her nipples. She needed the feel of his palms gliding across her skin, caressing the secret places that made her pussy wet. She needed to feel—alive.

His lips sought the sensitive spot behind her ear and tremors racked her body. Masculine palms shook slightly as they swept across her back, pulling her tight against him. The feel of his lips, his kisses trailing down her neck, released another surge of wetness between her thighs. She ached for him to fill her.

Lacy's fingernails dug into Wyatt's ass, driving his cock against her pussy. Her body writhed in his arms. There was a hunger in her touch, a need to devour. Her breath was raspy, desperate. She wanted it fast, hard, wild. Not the gentle loving he'd planned. With a quick swipe of a hand, Wyatt lifted her into his arms and headed for the bed.

She clung to him, her teeth grazing across his neck before nipping gently. Her heart pounded against his chest, beating out the rhythm of her need. He knew this because his own pulse, his own need, matched hers. They were in perfect sync when they hit the mattress.

The bed groaned beneath their weight as they rolled and struggled, each fighting the other for dominance. Her need to control the pace of their loving was evident as she guided his hand between her legs. He obliged her by pressing two fingers deep inside her.

She was wet, hot as he stroked her swollen lips. But he, too, needed something. He needed to hear her scream out his name, to beg him to pleasure her.

With one hand, he pinned her wrists above her head.

A soft growl floated from her parted lips. "I need to touch you." She squirmed beneath him.

"Not yet." In truth, he didn't know how long he could last if she touched him.

From the nightstand, he retrieved a necktie he'd left there last night. He wrapped the tie once around her wrists and watched her eyes widen, darken. When he looped the silk through the headboard her body arched into his. She moaned. Her eyelashes fluttered and then lay in dark crescents upon her cheeks.

What drove Wyatt, he didn't know, but it was a fantasy he had seen in his head more than once with Lacy. By the rapid rise and fall of her chest, she was as excited as he. This was how he had pictured her last night. Naked, stretched out on his bed, bound for his pleasure. In his dreams her legs were spread wide.

"Lacy, I'm going to tie your ankles to my bedposts." Breathlessly, he awaited her response. He nearly came when her laden voice croaked, "Anything, Wyatt, just fuck me. Fuck me now." Her hips rose as he climbed from the bed.

From the closet he extracted two more ties. They were his favorites, they'd be ruined after he got through with them, but they were being sacrificed for a worthy cause.

When he turned to approach the bed, Lacy's eyes were filled with dark desire.

He didn't speak as he wrapped a tie around one of her ankles. He left a little play so her knees could bend as he fastened the silk to a bedpost. Then he repeated the same process on her other foot. When she was spread-eagled, he climbed atop the bed, his cock aching so badly he thought he'd explode.

"Wyatt, I need you now." Her lithe body arched, her legs shaking as if a cold wind stroked her flesh.

If he touched her now, he was a goner.

When he rolled off the bed, Lacy's eyes inched wider. "Where are you going? Wyatt, *please*." The longing in her voice thrilled him.

He bent and kissed her lips. "Patience, baby, I have something you might like."

Lacy couldn't believe she had just let Wyatt tie her to his bed. She'd never done anything like this before, but she had to admit, it was a turn-on. She was so wet that once he took her, he'd be swimming in her juices. Just the thought of his thick cock driving in and out of her pussy made her body go up in flames.

With her wrists and ankles bound, excitement filled her. She *couldn't* touch him.

For the first time a sliver of apprehension took the place of excitement. Where had he gone? What did he plan to do to her? Before she could have further misgivings, he entered with a brandy snifter and warmer in one hand, a small bottle in the other. He set the items down on the nightstand. Then he sat on the edge of the bed, his back facing her.

While his broad shoulders hid what he was doing, she could hear glass tinkling and the quiet movements he made. But, when she heard a hiss and smelled sulfur, she couldn't remain quiet. "Wyatt?"

"Shhh, this will only take a minute."

"What?"

"Shhh. I promise you'll like it."

When he finally turned around, he had the brandy snifter in his hand. In slow circles he swirled a golden liquid in the snifter as he climbed upon the bed and straddled her. The head of his cock nudged against her pussy and she could have sworn her swollen lips opened, inviting him in.

He tipped the glass and the amber liquid spilled between her breasts. She gasped at the feel of the warm oil sliding down her skin. The scent of almonds rose.

A devilish smile curved Wyatt's lips as he began to spread the oil over her breasts. His palms smoothed the slick substance, teasing her nipples and kneading her flesh. Lightning bolts zinged through her pussy as his movements pushed his thick erection further inside her.

Her hips arched to take him deeper, but he rose onto his knees, depriving her of the fullness her body screamed for.

"Wyatt, *please*." She hated the whiny sound of her voice. Yet at that moment she'd do anything for him to fuck her.

"Shhh, baby, not yet." He reached for the snifter, the small flame under the burner flickered as he raised the glass and positioned it over the nest of hair at the juncture of Lacy's thighs. He tilted the glass and the oil rolled over the edge. Drip by drip the liquid soaked into her, warm against her skin, tantalizing as it began to slide lower toward her sex. When the slick substance reached her clit, tremors shook her. But it was the touch of his fingertips that sent her over the edge. She gasped, needing to touch him, but her bindings stopping her. Her body convulsed, lost to sensation—lost to the man hovering above her.

In one quick movement he entered her, pressing his body to hers. Her inner muscles squeezed him as he glided over her heated flesh, his cock sliding in and out of her pussy. The oil acted as a lubricant, moving them like a fine-tuned machine, as one.

She pulled at her wrists, her hands aching to caress him, to cradle him.

Her knees rose, he went deeper, harder. She screamed as another climax struck with a vengeance. Before she realized it, Wyatt joined her, ejaculating deep into her. As her hips jerked, milking the last of his semen, she reveled at the feel of his hot, wet seed in her body. Then she froze.

"Wyatt!" She jerked so hard against her bindings they came loose. "Wyatt!"

"Mmmm...what?" His sated voice was almost inaudible. He nibbled lightly on her neck.

"Please tell me you're wearing a condom."

He tensed above her. The silence was so thick you could cut it with a knife. He rolled over, lying on his back. "Sorry," he murmured.

"Sorry?" She went rigid. How could she have been so stupid? She jumped up from the bed and headed to the bathroom. She needed to wash up, and then say a very big prayer.

Wyatt knew he had fucked up as Lacy's form disappeared behind the bathroom door. She had a very ill child who needed her attention. An unplanned pregnancy was the last thing either of them needed — or wanted.

As she entered the bedroom, he slowly propped his head on a palm. His other hand pushed through his hair. He forced a smile and reached for her, but she dodged his grasp. "Come here."

She refused, backing away. "No."

He straightened into a sitting position, his legs hanging over the bed's edge, feet touching the floor. "Dammit, Lacy, I said I was sorry. Now, come here."

"No." He half expected her to stomp her foot.

He narrowed his eyes. "Don't make me come and get you." He must have placed just enough threat in his tone, as she hesitantly moved forward into his open arms.

"I'm not making light of the situation, but what's done is done. We'll face the consequences together."

She frowned down at him. "But—"

"No buts. I'm not your ex-husband, Lacy. I won't abandon you." Her frown deepened. The back of his hand smoothed across her cheek, hoping to chase away the hard lines etched around her lips. "Now let's climb into that warm bath together."

"I can't just brush this off."

He buried his face between her breasts and placed a kiss upon her soft skin. Then his gaze rose to meet hers. "Can you do anything about it right now?"

She didn't answer him.

"I didn't think so. Then let's enjoy tonight. From now on my sword will wear the shield of death. I promise."

She laughed. Her soft fingers stroked his body tenderly.

"I love your laugh." He hadn't meant to speak out loud, but was glad he had when she blushed a delightful pink. "C'mon, I want to bathe you." He rose, leading her to the bathroom.

Wyatt climbed in first, letting the warm water engulf him as he sat. Lacy moved between his legs, her back resting against his chest. For a moment he breathed in the light herbal scent of her hair.

A daddy. All his life he'd run fast and furious to keep from being trapped into marriage. There was no trap here. He was the guilty party. A woman tied to a bed couldn't be blamed. He had been in control and he'd fucked up.

She turned her head and gazed up at him. He kissed her soft lips. A shadow flickered in her eyes.

"So you're into bondage. What else? S&M?" There was a hesitant tone to her voice.

An unexpected chuckle burst from his mouth. "Actually, this was my first bondage experience. You bring out something wild and untamed in me. I want to bind you. Make your blood boil 'til you want me and me alone." He cupped her breasts. Gently, he rolled her nipples between his fingers.

It was the damnedest thing, but he wanted her. He'd only known this woman for a week. Still, he wanted her with a passion that danced along the edge of obsession.

When she turned in his arms, melding her body to his, he looked into her eyes. This was the woman he wanted to spend the rest of his life with. Ridiculous as it sounded, he knew it, sure as hell.

But would *she* have *him*?

Chapter Fifteen

ജ

Morning arrived and once again Lacy woke with her body on fire. She'd dreamed that she made love to Wyatt all night long. Even now, she could feel his mouth between her legs, stoking her desire.

Warm hands caressed her thighs, slipping beneath her ass to raise her for better penetration. She relaxed, giving in to the exquisite feel of his tongue deep inside her.

It wasn't a dream.

"Mmmm…" She stretched her arms, her body arching as she reached up. The room was dim, she could barely see Wyatt's eyes as his head rose. But she heard his low baritone voice slip across her heated skin.

"I was hungry."

"I can see that. Don't let me keep you from your breakfast." She spread her legs wide, eager for him to finish what he'd started.

Her breasts ached, her nipples burned. She grasped each taut nub between her fingers and pinched as Wyatt sucked her clit between his teeth and bit lightly. Lightning stung through her breasts, as fire raced through her womb toward her belly. She came quickly, unexpectedly, writhing as she released a low groan that felt like it had been ripped from deep inside her body.

As the last of her tremors subsided, Lacy was caught between pain and pleasure as Wyatt continued his assault. His tongue drove deeper. He ravished her folds, drinking in her juices like a starving man.

She twisted, pushing at his head. He gave no heed to her reaction. She was so sensitive, her nerve endings so raw, she'd die if he didn't stop.

"Wyatt, *please*, I can't take any more." When he rose, her sex was still pulsing, her hips squirming to assuage the pang.

"Then it's my turn." For a big man, he was lissome, sleek and sensuous, moving like a cat. The predatory gleam in his eyes made her catch her breath, but it was his wolfish grin that made her smile. A tendril of wavy black hair fell over his eyes. Dark eyelashes hung heavy. He was gorgeous.

His head dipped and he licked a path of fire from her bellybutton to the sensitive spot between her breasts. Her nipples beaded with anticipation. His smile grew as he watched them pucker, straining against her skin. In a swirling motion, his tongue swept over a taut peak.

Lacy's chest arched into his mouth, wanting him to take her deep. He responded by cupping her breast and taking in a heady mouthful, sucking, pulling and biting. His tongue danced across her aching nipple, then his body bowed and she felt the head of his cock nudge her swollen lips. He was still playing with her breast when he entered her.

He was rock-hard as he delved deep, groaning when he touched the end of her pussy. "God, baby, you feel good. So tight, warm and wet." His hips moved, increasing the rhythm.

It felt good, *too* good. "Wyatt, does your sword have a shield?" Lacy hated to interrupt the moment, but last night they had tempted fate enough.

Disheartened, he collapsed atop her. She groaned as his weight pushed her down into the bedding.

"Shit." It was all he said as he lay quietly atop her. The beat of his heart pounded against her chest. Then he did a push-up that relieved her of his upper body pressure. Aggravation blazed across his eyes. "Lacy, we have to do something about this. I'm suffocating in those damn things."

He looked so frustrated that she thought laughter a little inappropriate. Still, she couldn't resist teasing him. "Over-exaggerating just a little?"

"Fuck, Lacy, I want to feel the leather when I ride, not bang my head against a wall."

Her mouth opened and a burst of laughter rolled out. She'd never heard it put in quite that way, yet she knew exactly what he meant.

"I'm glad you find this funny." He climbed off the bed. His erection led the way as he stomped off, his bare feet slapping against the tile.

Her laughter died. "Wyatt?"

He ignored her as he began to rummage through a dresser drawer. When he slammed it shut, she started.

"Shit!"

Lacy raised into a sitting position. "What's wrong?"

He faced her. He was all hard muscle and sex appeal. She couldn't keep her eyes off the delicious cock arched proudly against his belly.

"No condoms."

In a heap of frustration she fell back upon the bed, her head landing on the soft pillow. He was right. If they were going to keep this affair going she would have to go back on the pill. Then she blinked hard. What was she saying? For a moment, she had lost sight of their situation. Not to mention she could already be pregnant. The thought made her stomach churn. She didn't need this complication now — or ever, for that matter.

The bed creaked as he sat on the edge, then he rolled over to take her in his arms. His hand pushed between her thighs, his fingers gliding across her slick folds.

She stilled his hand, wanting him, but knowing what was right. "We can't."

He tensed, his body rigid against hers. "I know." He released a frustrated breath. "I just need to touch you."

She pulled herself from his arms. "No. I'm not willing to take the chance of this getting out of control again."

A flood of emotion washed over her face. "I could already be pregnant." Her voice rose to a high pitch. "And...and what about my job?" She slid off the bed and looked down at him. "What about Jessie?"

"Calm down, Lacy."

Lacy's mouth gaped wide. She spun around and disappeared into the bathroom. Wyatt should have known that telling a woman concerned about her ailing child — and the possibility of another — to "calm down" was stupid. He needed to approach this problem in a different manner. But, how?

He pinched the bridge of his nose and closed his eyes. He didn't have all the answers right now. Somehow he would make it work. That was his job, to make impossible things happen.

When Lacy exited the bathroom she refused to meet his eyes. It was getting late and he still needed to feed the livestock and get ready for work. As he slipped on a pair of jogging pants and a t-shirt, his stomach growled. He hadn't eaten last night and was paying for it as hunger gnawed unmercifully at his backbone.

He brushed by her as he walked out of the bedroom.

The horses were neighing their hunger as he approached the stalls. Ace impatiently pawed the ground, then the damn animal tossed his head until Wyatt threw the flake of hay he held in his hands.

The cattle were a little more subdued and appreciative of his offerings. After he poured their feed into the bin, he leaned on the fence and watched them dig in.

When had his life gotten so complicated? He looked toward the house and knew the answer.

Well, he was burning daylight avoiding the inevitable. If they didn't get past their differences before they left for work, the issues would have to simmer until this evening. He pushed away from the fence and headed toward the house.

The minute he stepped inside the house the smell of sausage assaulted his senses. Lacy had found the kitchen. Nose in the air, he followed the heavenly scent. He stopped, spellbound, when he saw Lacy decked out in one of his t-shirts, standing before the stove, spatula in hand, turning potatoes.

Wyatt couldn't help himself. He strolled over to her, wrapped his arms around her waist and nuzzled her neck. "It smells almost as good as you do." She didn't pull away so he took more liberties, stroking his palms along her thighs and inching the shirt up, surprised and delighted to discover she wore nothing beneath it.

A finger slipped into her heat as he ground his hips to her rounded ass.

"If you keep that up I'll burn your breakfast. Maybe you could make yourself useful and set the table. How do you like your eggs?"

"Sunny-side up." Well at least she wasn't still mad, he thought, as he went to the sink and washed his hands. He let her shirt slide down, then moved to the cabinet where he kept the plates.

Sausage and toast were already on the table. After arranging silverware, he retrieved two coffee cups and filled them, the bitter aroma overwhelming his senses as he took a drink and sat down.

A few minutes later, Lacy placed the potatoes on the table and then set three eggs in front of him, the yellow yolks bright against glossy whites. Her own plate had only one egg, cooked over easy.

Wyatt dug into the feast. A piece of sausage disappeared into his mouth. "Mmmm. Damn good, thanks." He reached for a slice of toast.

She sipped quietly at her coffee.

After he put away all three eggs, two pieces of toast, a half pound of sausage and most of the potatoes, he noticed she hadn't eaten much of anything. A worried expression creased her forehead as she pushed her egg around the plate.

"Lacy, I'm not going to tell you that our situation isn't a difficult one. All we can do is take it one day at a time. We'll come up with something." He reached across the table and cupped his hand over hers. "Just don't give up before we have a chance."

Her gaze rose and he saw defeat in her eyes. "I don't have the luxury of making a mistake, Wyatt." She pulled her hand away and pushed from the table, her chair scraping across the floor. Silently, she began to clear the table.

He rose, carrying his plate and coffee cup to the sink. He ran the dishes under the water and handed them to

Lacy as she placed them into the dishwasher. She added the soap, closed the door and switched the machine on.

As she turned to leave, Wyatt grabbed her by the arm and pulled her into his embrace.

"Please?" was all he asked of her.

She nodded against his chest, her fingers curling into his shirt. Her head rose and he pressed his mouth to hers briefly. Her fingers clenched tighter, desperate.

His hand found the cheeks of her ass and he playfully swatted her. She jumped and squealed.

"Get dressed and don't take all day. We'll be late for work."

She gave him a wary half smile, stepping from his arms. His hand stilled her. He pulled her back against his chest and tasted her lips because he had to. When he released her this time, she glided toward the door and disappeared from the kitchen.

Wyatt briskly rubbed his palms together as he headed for the bedroom. Okay, this was good. Now all he had to do was come up with a plan that would meet all their needs, because there was no way in hell he would let her go.

Sitting on the bed, he slipped his shoes on as he watched Lacy move around his bedroom. It had been a while since a woman graced his house. He hadn't wanted any of them to stay longer than a weekend. Lacy he couldn't get enough of.

"Ready?" he asked, rising.

She tugged at her skirt and brushed a palm over her hair, ensuring it stayed in its severe knot.

"You really should wear your hair down more often. It's beautiful."

She picked up her purse. "But not professional."

He shook his head. "Lacy, just be yourself."

She raised a brow. "Is that how you climbed as far as you have?"

Well, she had him there. Business was a stage, its players characters in a performance. The curtain could rise and present you as the company's fair-haired child, or come crashing down and smash you in seconds. Everything you'd built throughout the years — status and career — could be gone in a heartbeat.

Wyatt needed to square up this thing with Lacy quickly or he ran the risk of seeing his career go up in smoke. He'd talk to HR today about relocating Lacy.

"C'mon, baby, let's hit the road," he said, holding open the door as they left the bedroom and then the house.

Both remained quiet as they walked toward the truck. He opened his door, forcing her next to him. Lacy didn't fight him when he tucked her in the curve of his arm. He put the vehicle in gear and pressed the accelerator.

As they approached the onramp at US-60, Lacy warned, "You're going to wreck if you don't keep your eyes off my legs."

He grinned. "But they're so damn sexy. In fact, spread 'em and let me imagine my hand smoothing over your skin, sliding a finger into your wet, warm pussy." He pressed his hand between her knees and attempted to pry them open.

Lacy squirmed, squeezing her legs tightly together. "Wyatt, stop it." She slapped at his roving hand.

Her halfhearted laugh made him smile. "Kiss me."

Her gaze snapped to his. "What?"

A small white car crossed the lane in front of them. Wyatt had to swerve to miss the sonofabitch. "Kiss me."

Traffic was heavy. The freeway was always congested heading westbound at seven in the morning. There wasn't six feet between the car in front of him and still he needed to touch her.

She shook her head, feigning disgust, but he saw the light in her eyes. "You're crazy."

"No, horny. Kiss me, Lacy."

She rolled her eyes. "You're not going to give up?"

"Not unless you kiss me."

She leaned into him, pressing her warm lips to his cheek.

"That's not a kiss. I want some tongue." Wyatt hit the brakes, throwing both of them forward as traffic came to a sudden stop. "Okay, if you don't give me a real kiss now you owe me a favor later, agreed?"

She grinned, sensing she'd won. "Okay. Now keep your eyes on the road."

The closer they came to Dunbar Semiconductors the more antsy Lacy got. She tugged at her skirt, slipping away from him, moving closer to the passenger door. He didn't comment or try to stop her. For now it was best to keep their relationship under wraps.

Wyatt maneuvered his truck into a parking space right next to Connie Smith's car.

She was still in it.

Through the vehicle's window he saw her graying brows rise, a smirk creeping across her weathered face.

So much for keeping their affair secret. Even though he could simply say he'd given Lacy a ride because of her car, the rumors would fly by the end of the day. Connie would make sure of that. He needed to do something, and quick.

Lacy hadn't seen Connie yet, and if he had his way she wouldn't. He took wide strides to hurry them along, knowing that Connie would have a shitload of stuff to carry in. She thought it was important to look like she took work home. It was all for show, as her duties weren't any more taxing than any of the other administrators.

"Did you call the hospital?" He swiped his ID badge. Before entering the revolving doors, he glanced over his shoulder at Connie struggling with her load. Standing just inside, he waited for Lacy to enter.

"Yes." She smiled, relief flowing across her face. "Jessie did fine last night."

"Do you want me to take you to see her at lunch?"

"No, the doctor is calling me around ten. I'll need a ride to pick up my car, if it's ready. Do you think it'll be fixed by then?"

"It depends on what's wrong with it. I'll call the dealership after nine." His voice softened. "Will you stay with me tonight?"

"Wyatt." He heard the exasperation in her voice.

"I'll make it worth your while."

"We'll see." She rolled her eyes again, shaking her head.

When they reached the top of the stairs she went her way, he went his.

Straight to Personnel.

Chapter Sixteen

ഔ

Raymond Travis sat behind his desk, his small frame hunched. Plaques and awards graced the wall behind him. He pinched the bridge of his nose. After what Wyatt had just told him about his relationship with Lacy, the man was speechless. Then he gazed up at Wyatt. "You trust her?"

"Yes." Wyatt responded without thinking. Yes, he did trust her. There was nothing deceptive about Lacy. He shifted his weight in the chair, swallowing hard.

The HR manager leaned forward. "Body language speaks loudly, DW. What?"

"She's concerned about her job. She has a sick kid. Raymond, she *needs* this job."

Raymond scooted his chair further beneath his desk. "You know the rules. She can't work for you."

"Then find her somewhere else to work."

"There aren't any openings right now. Upper management just put a freeze on hiring. You know that."

Tension gathered in the tendons of Wyatt's neck. His palm rubbed at the ache, but it remained. This wasn't going how he'd planned. "Switch her with one of the other newbies."

Waves of brown hair shifted as the man's head bobbed. "That might be a possibility. Let me make a couple of inquiries. But I suggest you keep this under wraps in the meantime."

Too late. Wyatt rubbed his now-throbbing temples.

The man laid his pen down upon his desk, as he took in Wyatt's weary expression. "What?"

"Her car broke down. I gave her a ride to work and, well, Connie Smith saw us drive up."

Raymond released a breath of disbelief and leaned back in his chair. "Of all the people. DW, I can call her in and have a talk with her, but it might make things worse. Until she does something inappropriate, legally, I can't take any action."

Frustration heated Wyatt's face. "Damn it, Raymond, its Lacy's reputation that'll take the hit."

The small man shook his head. He eased off his glasses. Using a tissue he swiped both lenses. When he settled them on his nose again, he pinned Wyatt with a no-nonsense glare.

"Unless you're willing to break this thing off, there isn't any other choice. Even then, the damage will be done."

"Fuck!" Wyatt leaned forward and buried his face in his palms. What would Lacy say when the shit hit the fan? And it was just a matter of time before it did.

Abruptly he stood. "Relocate her." His tone was short, decisive. Without another word, he headed for the door. He was already late for a meeting, and Lacy was supposed to be there.

When he reached the conference room near his office, Wyatt scanned the room. Lacy had yet to arrive. John and Carl were seated at the large mahogany table, giving him a nod as he entered. Several staff members were bidding for choice seats next to them. Chatter rose as more employees entered.

He took a seat with open chairs on each side of him, praying that Lacy would arrive before he was bombarded by employees eager to share their latest discovery or idea with him. It wasn't to be. Larry, the product engineer Lacy was assigned to assist, took one seat and Adam, a design engineer, sat in the other. The only seat available when Lacy arrived was one across from him.

Her gaze darted around the room before she scooted the chair out and sat down. Their eyes met briefly as his cell phone went off. He glanced at the caller ID. It was the dealership returning his earlier call regarding Lacy's car.

"Excuse me. I need to take this." Wyatt rose and left the room. After five minutes he returned, having told the serviceman to make what repairs were necessary. He'd been right. The alternator was draining the battery. The car also needed several belts and hoses, including an alignment, not to mention new tires. He hadn't had time to confer with Lacy. Either way, he intended to pay for the repairs.

When he returned, he chanced a glance in Lacy's direction. She looked nervous as she squirmed in her seat, working way too hard not to look at him.

A warm feeling seeped into his bones as he watched her. Then she turned, their gazes met, and she smiled. The connection sent a zap of desire straight to his cock. The material across his groin tightened. He wanted her. If she'd sat next to him, he would have shown her just how much with a stolen touch beneath the table.

As John stood up to present, Lacy glanced at Wyatt.

What would the people around the table say if they knew his thoughts? What would happen if he stripped Lacy naked and took her right here, before their eyes? The thought of Lacy naked drew his balls tight. He shifted in his seat, aching with the need to delve between her thighs, to bathe in her warmth.

Heaviness tugged at his groin. He had to spread his thighs, seeking a comfortable position to ease the lust that swamped him. He wanted her with a passion too powerful to restrain. So deep he felt like he was drowning. It was overwhelming and almost frightening in its intensity.

Pinning his gaze on John, he knew he had to rein in his desire. Still, he couldn't resist a glance in Lacy's direction. The most delightful shade of pink colored her cheeks. Her chest rose and fell deeply. What was going through her mind? Did she want him as much as he did her?

One presenter after the other spoke until finally the meeting ended. It was fifteen minutes before noon as everyone filtered out of his office, including Lacy.

Leisurely, he sat behind his desk and scanned through the numerous emails. Fifteen minutes and he would take Lacy to pick up her car, maybe even indulge in a little afternoon delight before they returned to work.

When the door opened, Wyatt looked up from his computer.

Raymond Travis stood there, grinning.

Wyatt held his breath. "You found something?"

Raymond nodded as he took a seat. "Wireless actually had a newbie renege. He took a position with another company."

Wyatt frowned. "Wireless is in Chandler." He'd hoped for something at this facility. Now they wouldn't be able to drive to work together. He wouldn't be able to steal a kiss, a caress.

"DW, it's all we've got. I spoke with Bob Henderson and he's excited about having her join his team. He remembers her from the engineering fair at ASU. Actually, he extended her an offer."

"I bet." Wyatt's tone was laden with disappointment and suspicion. "Well—"

"Wyatt?" Lacy's soft voice whispered before she stuck her head around the corner into his office. "Oh, excuse me." She turned to leave.

"No wait. Come join us." As she moved further into the room, Raymond rose and closed the door behind her. "I've got good news."

Lacy's bewildered gaze went from Raymond to Wyatt and then back again. "Good news?"

"I've found you another position," Raymond said proudly as he sat down.

Lacy's eyes nearly popped out of their sockets. "*What?*"

Raymond squirmed in his chair. "Uh, I...uh, DW, didn't you discuss this with her?" He cleared his throat nervously.

Wyatt could almost feel the daggers shooting from her eyes. She trembled. Her fingers curled into fists. Her mouth opened, then shut, then opened again.

"Thank you." Her voice shook with unspoken rage. Then she glanced at Wyatt. "Thank you," she said more firmly. "When do I start?"

Wyatt watched the tension drain from Raymond's body. A weak smile curved his lips. "This afternoon, if you're available?"

"I'm available." She turned to Wyatt. "I suppose you'll handle this with Carl, since you've been so good at handling everything else in my life." She spun around and jerked open the door, slamming it behind her.

Raymond's attempts to speak were brushed off with a wave of Wyatt's hand. "She's fine. Just finish the deal," he said pushing past the stunned man.

Damn the woman. Didn't she know he was doing this for them? Wyatt was worried, but knew they could work through it. They had to.

* * * * *

Lacy was shaking so bad that when she reached for her purse she knocked a pile of papers on the floor. She bent to retrieve them as the telephone rang. She thought to ignore it. Instead, she pressed the receiver to her ear, and took a deep breath before speaking.

"Dunbar Semiconductors, this is Lacy."

"Ms. Mason this is Dr. Lawrence. Good news."

It was the second time today she had heard those two words. *Good for whom*, she wondered?

"The United Network for Organ Sharing has a heart for Jessie."

As if every bone in her body dissolved, she felt her anger melt. Slowly, she sank into her chair. "But, I thought..."

"Due to the size of the donor's heart, the patient ahead of Jessie was not a good candidate."

It was happening. Jessie was getting a new heart. Lacy attempted to swallow the lump in her throat, succeeding only in making it feel larger as she struggled to inhale.

"We're currently running the necessary tests. Ms. Mason, do you understand?"

Lacy nodded.

"Ms. Mason?"

"Yes," her response was barely audible.

"A social worker by the name of Laura Sinclair will be at the surgical wing on the second floor awaiting you. You need to come immediately."

"Yes." She was still holding the receiver with no one on the other line when Wyatt entered her cubicle.

Wyatt squared his shoulders, preparing for the resistance he expected from Lacy. Hopefully, she wouldn't coldcock him in front of everyone. The damn woman would just have to compromise, because he wouldn't give her up.

When their eyes met, Wyatt froze. He knew that desperate, haunted look. The frantic expression could only mean one thing.

Jessie.

He reached out and touched Lacy's shoulder, giving it a little squeeze. "I'll drive you."

She nodded.

Lacy stood for only a second, before she grabbed her purse and flew past him. He followed. They rushed down the stairs and through the halls to exit the facility. In a flash, they were in Wyatt's truck and down the road.

When Lacy had opened the passenger side door and climbed into the truck, Wyatt sensed she needed her space. Yet he wanted to hold her, feel her warmth next to him. It was important that she realize he was there for her. He couldn't bear her silence, nor the pain wrenched across her face. It was more than he could take.

Wyatt patted the seat beside him. "Lacy, come here."

She frowned and shook her head.

"C'mon, baby," he coaxed.

He knew the minute her composure shattered. Tears seeped from her eyes as she scooted next to him, folding herself against his side. He draped an arm over her shoulder and held her close. Heard the heavy gust of air that left her lungs before deep, heart-wrenching sobs shook her body. He tightened his grip.

"What happened?"

She hiccupped, rummaging through her purse. She brought a tissue to her nose and wiped. "They found a donor. Jessie's going into surgery."

"What! Now?"

All she could do was nod.

Stunned, Wyatt maneuvered his truck onto the I-10 and headed north.

Several miles down the road Lacy had finally reeled in her emotions. But Wyatt was sure they lingered just below the surface, fragile, nearing the breaking point.

"Lacy, what exactly is wrong with Jessie?"

"She has idiopathic cardiomyopathy."

Wyatt had heard of cardiomyopathy, a disease of the heart muscle in which the heart loses its ability to pump blood effectively.

"A year ago she became ill...and was diagnosed." Lacy blinked hard. "The doctor said that seventy-nine percent of pediatric cardiomyopathy occurs for some unknown reason. Idiopathic—unknown..." Her voice faded away. Silently, she stared out the window.

When she turned and spoke again, her tone was eerily soft. "Heart transplant patients have a ninety percent chance of making it past one year." She bit down hard on her bottom lip, leaving teeth imprints when she released it. Moisture spiked her eyelashes. "But the longest surviving heart recipient only lived for seventeen years after the transplant. That was in 1986." She gazed up at him, blinking rapidly to keep tears at bay. "If my baby lives through this she might only have a few years, maybe only seventeen at the most."

"Don't think that way, Lacy. Medical science is improving every day." He held her tighter, wanting to drive the doubt from her mind, but not knowing how. He

205

needed to embrace her fully, but also needed to stay on the road as they passed one vehicle after another in their haste.

Neither spoke after that, until they reached the hospital.

"Shit!" Wyatt barked.

Parking was awful. With each aisle he drove down, Lacy shifted anxiously on the seat. Finally, he saw a white truck pulling out in front of them. He pulled close, easing into the spot. When he shifted into park, Lacy began to tremble.

"Breathe, sweetheart." He grasped her chin and drew her gaze to his. Dark desperation was reflected back at him. Gently, he pressed his lips to hers. "Everything is going to be fine." He gave her chin a little shake before releasing her and opening the truck door, hoping he was right.

Lacy's feet hit the ground running.

As they entered the hospital, Wyatt drew Lacy next to him, slowing her pace. The last thing either of them needed was to slip and fall on the newly waxed floor. Lights glistened off the polished linoleum. The smell of the cleaning agent that had been used still lingered in the air, mixed with the antiseptic scent of the hospital.

God, he hated hospitals. He grasped her hand and trudged on.

The elevator ride was short as they headed toward the surgical wing. The distance down the hall even shorter. He felt Lacy tense beneath his hand as they neared the room with Jessie inside. The door was shut. She stopped, motionless, unable to take the next step. So he did it for her. Wrapping his arm around her, he pushed open the door, stepped inside, dragging her with him.

A crowd of people surrounded the bed. When they parted, a pale but cheery little girl yelled, "Mommy!"

Lacy went weak in his arms. Her body eased out of his grasp, eager to see her daughter. He released her and she walked calmly into the crowd. He knew her composure and the forced smile cost her dearly. Had he been the only one to see her misstep, her sway before she folded her arms around Jessie?

"Hey, baby." Her voice sounded hearty, as if it was just another day. For her daughter, she would shield her emotions. Quietly she held the little girl who looked so much like her.

Something indescribable shook Wyatt. This woman was the epitome of strength, of courage, of *love*. She would fight with every fiber in her body and soul to save the ones she loved. He wanted to be in her circle of loved ones, if only she would let him.

Breathe. Such an easy command, still Lacy felt her lungs lock up, refuse to take air. She had to be strong for Jessie. She couldn't let her daughter see her fear. When a warm hand slipped around her waist, a gasp of air flowed in through her mouth, filling her lungs.

Wyatt.

Just knowing he was here—that he *wanted* to be here with her—was comforting. She released Jessie and drew Wyatt closer. "Jessie, this is Mr. Anderson, h-he's a friend."

"Hi." Jessie snuggled shyly into Lacy's side.

Wyatt extended his hand. "Hi, Jessie. It's a pleasure to finally meet you." Jessie's little hand disappeared in Wyatt's large one. Lacy smiled. She couldn't help herself as she watched them together.

"Ms. Mason." Dr. Lawrence drew her attention. "The surgical staff and I have been visiting with Jessie." Jessie smiled up at the doctor. He returned the gesture with ease. "I've explained to her what we'll be doing."

Lacy frowned. Surely not.

"I mean to say, that this nice lady, Dr. Carter," Lacy turned to acknowledge the short blonde dressed in green scrubs, "will be helping her to sleep, while Dr. Jamison and Dr. Stewart assist me in making her feel better."

Lacy released the breath she'd been holding as she nodded to Dr. Jamison, a tall distinguished-looking man, and then Dr. Stewart, who looked entirely too intense. Next to them was a willowy woman who was introduced as Laura Sinclair, the social worker, and Ms. Ferguson, the surgical nurse who would be looking after Jessie during the procedure.

A bolt of fear shook Lacy. This was real. Unconsciously, she reached behind her and grasped Wyatt's hand, an anchor in the raging storm that was threatening to engulf her. She hadn't thought she needed anyone except Jessie. But she needed Wyatt. If she was to survive this ordeal, she'd take whatever he offered.

"While Ms. Ferguson assists Jessie with her booties and cap, why don't we step outside and talk?" Dr. Lawrence moved toward the door.

In the hall, Dr. Lawrence explained the details and risks of the procedure, which Lacy knew all too well. Then he gathered her hands in his. "Ms. Mason, we'll take good care of Jessie. I don't see any reason why we won't be successful."

Again, Lacy found Wyatt's strong arm around her waist. His nod of confidence warmed her. Jessie would be all right. She just had to be.

In the waiting room, Wyatt called Dunbar and made their excuses. She heard him ask that they not bother him unless it was urgent. Then he turned to her and she went willingly into his open arms.

They waited.

The hours that passed were the longest of her life. Yet Lacy wasn't alone. She shared the time with Wyatt. Never once did he let her out of his sight, nor relinquish the arm he had around her.

When the door of the waiting room opened and Dr. Lawrence finally entered, Lacy's heart stopped.

Chapter Seventeen

The silence was deafening as Lacy and Wyatt came to their feet. Dr. Lawrence looked beyond exhausted. Weariness lined his reddened eyes as he scanned the crowded waiting room. When their eyes met, Lacy's breath caught.

"Ms. Mason." The heaviness in the doctor's voice weakened her knees. She began to collapse. Only the arm Wyatt slid around her waist kept her standing, her body leaning into him for support. "We're finished, but…"

The air felt brittle. Lacy's head filled with a gauzy substance that made all sounds dull, muffled and far away, except for the clock on the wall. The *tick – tick – tick*, thundered in her head. A warning that time was slipping away.

"…Jessie is weak. The next twenty-four hours are critical," the doctor finished.

Lacy couldn't speak. The questions she had mentally been prepared to ask, were gone—vanished like smoke in a strong wind.

"When can we see Jessie?" asked Wyatt, tugging Lacy to his side. He pressed his warm lips to her forehead.

"She'll be in recovery for a while. A nurse will come to get you when she's stabilized. Any questions?"

Wyatt looked down at her, his eyes searching for an answer Lacy didn't have. Her silence lingered. "Not at this time," he said.

The gray-haired doctor's hand covered Lacy's trembling one and squeezed. "Don't lose faith, Ms. Mason."

The air trapped in Lacy's lungs escaped in a single sigh. She couldn't stop the tears that began to stream down her cheeks. On a ragged inhale she gasped, choking on the emotion that refused to yield. The only things holding her together were Wyatt's arms as he embraced her, pressing her to his chest and hips. She prayed he wouldn't let go. If he did, she would crumble into a million pieces.

"I need to get back." Dr. Lawrence released Lacy's hand and left the room.

When the doctor disappeared, Lacy turned in Wyatt's arms, burying her face into his chest. The scent of his masculine cologne, the heat of his body, overtook her senses. He stroked her back and rocked her slightly, like a parent would comfort a child. She was reluctant to pull away. Still, Lacy took a small step backwards. Wyatt's palms slid down her arms to her hands. He cupped them tight in a show of support.

"I need to call Jay's mother. He should know…" *Would he care?* she wondered. How could he not?

Wyatt tensed and slowly released her.

Dammit. She didn't need this, not now. Jay was Jessie's father. He had a right to know.

Relief filtered through her when Wyatt nodded. "Coffee?" Before she could answer, he said, "I'll get you a cup while you make the call."

Wyatt left her standing alone as he headed for the small kitchenette in the far corner of the waiting room.

Settling into a chair, Lacy extracted her cell phone and began to punch in Ruth Mason's telephone number.

"Hello, Mason residence." Lacy's ex-mother-in-law's voice scratched across the wavelengths.

"Ruth, this is Lariat." Silence met Lacy's words. *God give me strength.* "Ruth, Jessie's just had a heart transplant. Can you please get a message to Jay?"

"And why weren't we called earlier?" snapped the woman.

Every nerve in Lacy's body tightened. "Because there wasn't time." She would not argue with this woman—not now. "Just let Jay know that we're at St. Joseph's Hospital. The next twenty-four hours are critical. He should be here."

"Well, little lady—"

Snap. Lacy closed the phone. She was blindly staring at the cell phone when Wyatt returned, two cups of steaming coffee in his hands. The strong smell assailed Lacy's nose as he handed her a cup.

"From the look on your face, it wasn't a pleasant call." Wyatt took the seat next to her.

"It's never a pleasant event with Jay's mother." Lacy sipped the coffee. Her face crinkled with distaste.

Wyatt chuckled. "Would you like me to get you another cup from the cafeteria?"

She set the offensive drink on the coffee table to her right. "No, just sit here with me." She gazed at his handsome face. They were virtual strangers, yet here this man sat, willingly extending his support.

He cradled his hot drink in his palms, blowing the steam from the cup. "What?"

Lacy struggled to put into words what his presence meant to her. In the end, she whispered, "Thank you."

Wyatt set his coffee down and pulled her onto his lap. His embrace was warm, strong, everything she needed.

"I—"

"Shhh. Just let me hold you, Lacy. Let me take care of you." Then he pressed his soft lips to hers, taking control.

It didn't matter that the room was full of people. A dozen or more eyes on them. Lacy would accept the comfort Wyatt offered, because she needed it. And more importantly, she wanted it.

* * * * *

At the break of dawn the next day, Jessie had finally been taken up to the Pediatric Intensive Care Unit. For over twelve hours Wyatt and Lacy watched the child's fragile body poked and prodded with needles and tubes. It was enough to bring a strong man to his knees, him included.

He couldn't imagine how Lacy was able to hold herself together. But she did. Her palm smoothed over her daughter's small hand, avoiding the intravenous line. Love shimmered from every pore of her body.

Lacy was incredible. A woman with a spine of steel. A woman Wyatt knew he had to have.

"Maybe we should go home, take a shower, get clean clothes on." His suggestion was met with a huff.

"I can't leave Jessie." She scooted her chair closer to the bed, as if preparing herself to fight him off if he insisted.

"Sweetheart, you need rest."

"No!" Her response was sharp. She inhaled, then released the air slowly. When their gazes met, she said, "You go. I can't leave Jessie."

Truth was, Wyatt had to get out of the hospital. The smell of antiseptic, the moans and cries of the other patients, the beeps of the equipment and the pain in Lacy's eyes was more than he could handle.

Men were supposedly stronger than women, but Lacy was putting him to shame.

"Why don't I go and get us something to eat? I can't stomach hospital food." Wyatt pushed from his worn chair. The imprint of his ass still lingered in the green vinyl.

Lacy forced a smile that didn't make it to her tired eyes. "Sure. That would be nice."

"Will you eat if I bring you something?"

She nodded. He doubted she meant it.

He stood. Her gaze scanned his body slowly and heat exploded through him. God, the woman drove him wild and she didn't even know it. Like a starving man, he pulled her from her chair and into his arms. Their mouths fused, their tongues meeting and intertwining. When he released her, she was breathless. He thought she would kiss him again, but then she glanced at her daughter and stepped away.

"Go. You need a break." She sensed his discomfort. But more importantly, the look of acceptance on her face said she understood.

Wyatt couldn't help it. He wove his fingers through her hair, cupping the nape of her neck, bringing her close. For a moment he simply gazed into her amber eyes. *I love you* was on the tip of his tongue. But that was irrational. He'd only known this woman for a matter of days.

He wasn't someone who fell in love quickly. Shit, he was an engineer. There was a process, procedures to follow. Time was required.

Before he could let the words slip from his mouth, he kissed her and left the room.

Chapter Eighteen

ಬ

The first sign of a problem was the warning alarm that screeched from the blood pressure monitor. Lacy sprang from her chair, her heart pounding against her chest.

Jessie was pale, so pale. The bright green lights glowed sixty-two, fifty-six. Her blood pressure was dropping rapidly.

Lacy reached for the call button, but already the emergency team was rushing through the door.

"Wh-what's happening?" Ushered from the room against her will by one of the night nurses, Lacy struggled, refusing to admit the obvious.

Jessie's new heart was failing.

When the doors closed, barring her from her precious baby, Lacy felt as if her own heart was stopping. A vise squeezed around her chest. Pain struck, so intense that her knees gave and she collapsed to the floor.

This can't be happening. Please, God, don't do this to me — to my child.

Was He listening? Would He answer her prayers?

"Lacy?" Someone was calling her name. "Lacy?"

When she had the strength to lift her head her ex-husband stood before her.

"Jay." Her voice was small.

"What's going on?" He grasped her arms and pulled Lacy to her feet.

"Jessie," was all she managed to say.

"Is she okay?" Lacy was surprised by the concern in his tone.

"No."

"Dammit, Lacy, what's going on?"

"Her heart is failing. They're working on her."

"Fuck." He tore off his Stetson and slammed it against his leg, before swiping his fingers through his hair.

Hot tears beat against Lacy's eyelids. "I can't live without her." The forsaken admission seeped from her trembling lips.

"I know, doll." Jay pulled her into his embrace.

It felt awkward in his arms. Where was Wyatt? She needed Wyatt.

Her pleas were answered as he appeared from around a corner. A brown bag was in his hands. The smile on his face faded as he came to abrupt stop.

Lacy attempted to pull from Jay's embrace, but his grasp tightened.

Wyatt's gaze darkened. She could see indecision warring in his eyes. When he pivoted, retracing his steps, Lacy's heart sank. She needed him now more than ever. She loved him.

Only after Wyatt was out of sight did Jay release her. She didn't need this now, not while her daughter fought for her very life. She wanted to run after Wyatt, explain what was happening, but she couldn't. She couldn't leave her daughter alone.

Lacy stared at the empty place where Wyatt had stood, frozen. She listened to the noises coming from Jessie's room. A numbing sensation was slowly taking over her body.

"Jay, how'd you get here so fast?" she managed to get out.

"Mom's message was waiting for me as my plane touched down."

Lacy slowly turned. Jay cared. He was returning to be with his daughter.

Then she saw the elbow brace and knew the truth. He'd gotten hurt and couldn't ride, that was the reason he was back. Returning to cause more havoc in hers and Jessie's lives.

"Leave, Jay." Finality sounded in her tired voice.

He took a step toward her. "But, Lacy—"

Her uplifted palm drew him to a halt. "Don't—don't you *Lacy* me. You only came back because you can't ride."

"I would have come for Jessie. For you."

"Oh would you?" Her words lingered as Jessie's door opened and a doctor waved Lacy into the room.

Wyatt's footsteps stamped his fury into the floor. His teeth ached from the pressure in his clenched jaws. He realized it wasn't anger. The jackhammer that had hit him square in the chest when he found Lacy in her ex-husband's arms had been disappointment, hurt. The need to tear the man's arms from around her was a red-hot fire in his gut. Yet Lacy was right. The man had a legitimate right to be here for his daughter.

Still, acceptance was far from Wyatt's reach. Lacy was his. Jessie should be *his* responsibility, not her absent father's.

Where that thought came from, he didn't know.

As Wyatt passed a trash can, he dumped the brown bag. Food was the farthest thing from his mind. The

217

automatic doors of the emergency room slid open and he wandered outside. He wouldn't leave the hospital. He had to know if both Jessie and Lacy were going to be okay. But right now he needed to put distance between himself and Lacy's ex.

But it wasn't to be. Jay Mason was hot on his trail and he didn't look any happier than Wyatt felt.

"I ought to kill you, you sonofabitch." Mason's voice was shaking, his face flushed.

Wyatt was prepared for an altercation. Although it wasn't the most appropriate time or place, he was ready to pummel the man standing before him.

"Why? For being there for Lacy and Jessie when you haven't?"

"You *stole* my family."

"No. You let them go. Tell me, man to man," they began to circle each other, "were you ever there for Lacy? Did you really love her? Or was she just a conquest? Are you prepared to take care of Jessie?" Mason slowed, then stopped. "She'll need constant medical care until she's recovered. And money... What about the expenses? Will you abandon them when it gets too hot to handle?"

When Mason turned away, his actions spoke for themselves. "Do you love her?"

Wyatt nodded. "Yes, I do."

Mason pivoted, his features tight with emotion. "You'll take care of my little girl?"

"The best I can," Wyatt replied.

"I'll kill you if you don't," Mason growled.

Wyatt smiled. "You can try."

"I left my number at the nurses' station. Have Lacy call me when she knows something. I'm going home." The man sounded deflated as he turned and walked away. Wyatt watched him climb into his rental car and drive off.

You stole my family. The man's words kept ringing through Wyatt's ears. What had given Mason that idea? Had Lacy said something to him?

Wyatt rushed through the sliding glass doors and headed for the elevator. The ride was excruciating—it seemed to take forever. He needed to be with Lacy, needed to hold her in his arms.

When he arrived at Jessie's room, Lacy wasn't in the hall, and the door was shut. Quietly, he pushed it open and stepped inside. A male nurse was fiddling with a tube as Lacy turned to face him. Her eyes were swollen with tears. She looked tired, worn-out. She took one step, then another, almost running into his open arms.

Lacy buried her face into his shoulder. "Where were you? I needed you." Her words warmed Wyatt.

"I'm here now, sweetheart." He felt her tremble.

"I almost lost her, Wyatt."

He held her tighter, stroked her hair. "I'm sorry, honey. I shouldn't have left. But I'm here now. I'll always be here."

"Excuse me," the male nurse interrupted as he moved around the bed. "Ms. Mason, I'll be with Jessie for a while if you need to get something to eat. I can call you if anything changes." His lips curved into a smile. "But I'm sure it won't."

"Wyatt brought something for us to eat," she said, as Wyatt's brows shot up. "Didn't you?"

"I...uh...well, maybe we should go to the cafeteria." Lacy glance of indecision toward Jessie made Wyatt continue, "We'll only be a short distance away from her. We need to talk."

With a little more persuasion, Lacy finally relented. Wyatt wrapped his arm around her shoulders and together they headed for the cafeteria.

The grill was closed. The only thing available was prepackaged sandwiches. The hamburgers sitting in the trash can outside were sounding more and more tempting.

Wyatt pulled out a chair for Lacy and she sat, blindly staring at the food in front of her.

"You need to eat." Wyatt sat next to her. He reached for Lacy's tuna salad sandwich and began to remove the cellophane. When he handed it to Lacy, she took a bite and set it down.

"What do we need to talk about?"

Wyatt shifted nervously in his chair. "Marry me."

Lacy's jaw dropped. Surely she hadn't heard Wyatt clearly. Had he just asked her to marry him?

"I know it seems sudden." Wyatt placed his hand over hers. "But I love you, and I want to take care of you and Jessie."

Lacy was stunned. He *had* asked her to marry him. She shook her head. Surely, he had no idea what he was getting into. "Living with a transplant is a lifelong process, Wyatt. Jessie will be on medications to trick her immune system, so that it doesn't attack the transplanted organ. There are medications she'll take just to prevent side effects of the anti-rejection medications. It will be a long haul, and expensive."

She paused, but he didn't appear troubled by her revelations. "In time, she'll be able to care for herself, but not now. I'm all she has." Tears glistened in Lacy eyes.

Wyatt scooted his chair closer, snaked his arm around her shoulders. "No, Lacy, *we're* all she has. You and me, along with my family and the brothers and sisters you and I will give her to play with."

Lacy couldn't help the thrill that ran through her.

"Say yes, Lacy."

Before she could answer he pressed his lips to hers.

Chapter Nineteen
One month later…

ᔀ

Lacy stretched, the silky sheets sliding over her naked body. She looked around Wyatt's bedroom — *their bedroom* — and smiled. Blindly, she reached behind her, palm patting empty space. Her grin faded as she rolled over to find Wyatt gone. Only the impression of his head remained in the pillow. The bedding had cooled. He'd been gone for some time.

As she pushed to a sitting position, Wyatt entered the room, pulled the door closed.

"Where —?"

"Shhh…" He pressed a finger to his lips. "Jessie woke up." Lacy swung a leg over the side of the bed and made to get up. "No," he insisted, his gaze scanning her appraisingly and causing the most decadent heat to roll across her skin. "I rocked her back to sleep." His dusky blue eyes darkened.

"Why didn't you wake me?"

Without a word, he untied the sash around his robe, shedding it with a single shrug of his broad shoulders. As it pooled at his ankles, he said, "I had other plans."

His naked body was magnificent. Golden skin stretched tight over well-defined muscles moved toward her. His eyes were pinned on her breasts.

Her nipples reacted immediately, tightening under his blatant perusal. His cock jerked, growing larger, harder, under her examination.

With a swipe of her tongue, she wet her lips in anticipation of his erection buried deep within her body, the slow rocking of their bodies, the unity of their souls.

"Scoot over," he said, sliding next to her. "It's time for mommy and daddy to play." His voice was heavy with desire.

Lacy slid over, lying on her back, as the bed creaked beneath his weight. So much had changed in the past month. Their wedding had been a quiet, quick event in the hospital chapel. Their days had fallen into a new schedule. Wyatt going to work each day, Lacy taking care of Jessie. Her job could wait until Jessie was better.

But, the nights…the nights were for the two of them.

Wyatt's palm curved around her breast and kneaded gently. She loved the feel of his hands on her skin. His other hand found the wet pulse between her thighs. He parted her folds, a single finger sinking between them.

He shuddered. The depth of his desire made her tingle with joy.

"I need to be inside you," he groaned, moving atop her, spreading her legs wide. His eyes were dark, hungry with need as he slid atop her, flesh to flesh. With a single thrust, he entered her.

Lacy gasped. Her back arched, hips rising to meet his. A tender ache spread across her as she looked up at him. She reached for him, his body hot and strong, smooth skin over hard muscle.

"I love you," he murmured, before bending and pressing his lips to hers. With slow strokes his hips pumped, driving his cock in and out of her moist core, while his tongue mated with her mouth. His hands caressed her body, outlining the dip of her waist, then resting on her hips as he lifted her and drove deeper.

"Wyatt!" Lacy couldn't help the cry that pushed from her lips as they parted and came back together. With each thrust he was building a fire within her that threatened to burn out of control. Her breasts were heavy, her slick folds cradling him as he moved in and out.

"I need more of you," he growled. Separating their bodies, he knelt so his ass rested on the back of his calves. "Straddle me." His breathing was labored. The roughness in his voice and the scent of their loving was heady. But it was his cock jutting proudly from the nest of hair between his thighs that made Lacy scramble to her hands and knees to take him into her mouth.

His throaty groan was enough to send another wave of electricity through her pussy. Her body felt alive, life coursing through every vein.

"Awww…ohhhh, baby." There was a brief pause. *"Stop! Stop!"* Another tremor made him shake all over. He clenched his eyelids and tensed, fighting the inevitable climax.

She released him, but not without flickering her tongue over the crown of his erection. He was still resting on his haunches as she spread her knees, straddling and mounting him, taking him deep within her body.

His hands went to her waist, fingers gripping, immobilizing. Still, she ground her hips, searching for that one spot that would set her off like a Roman candle.

They were both close to climaxing, as the rhythm of their loving increased. His cock thrusting, stretching her to a point where she thought she'd shatter… And then she did.

Bright light burst behind her eyelids. Her body convulsed, quaking with each delicious wave of sensation. Wyatt followed her into the abyss.

Never had Lacy felt such passion, such intensity. It bordered on obsession. This man was everything she had ever dreamt of—and he was all hers. As the heat of the moment cooled, Wyatt rolled them onto their sides, facing one another. He looked happy, content.

Propped up on an elbow, Wyatt's palm cradled his head as he looked into Lacy's golden eyes. Her beautiful breasts rose as she breathed softly, returning his gaze. There was a peaceful serenity to the moment.

God, she was beautiful. He couldn't help but touch her. His finger traced the tilt of her nose. "Jessie has your nose."

Lacy's smile beamed with pride. "It's the Dawn trademark. All the women in my family had the tilt. It goes along with our stubbornness."

"Is that a warning?" His palm caressed her neck, dipped in the crevice of her collarbone and moved across her chest, until he cupped her breast.

The beat of her heart sped beneath his touch. Her breath caught as he tweaked her nipple. "N-no. A promise."

He bent, drawing the taut bud in his warm mouth, and then bit. She yipped, wrapping her fingers in his hair. Blowing a long stream of air on the dampened skin, he watched the dark skin of her areola rise with small bumps. With the pad of his finger, he smoothed over the swell.

"I love touching you." His palm grazed her stomach, before resting on her mons. "And kissing you." His lips caressed the soft skin between her breasts, then feathered down her stomach. "And tasting you." He moved between her thighs, then stroked his tongue across her folds. She shivered beneath his touch, goose bumps rising over her stomach, arms and legs. "You taste like honey." He delved deeper, wrenching a moan from her lips.

As he circled her clit, she tightened her grasp on his hair. When he sucked the swollen nub into his mouth and nipped, her hips flew off the bed, writhing beneath his assault. His hands held her hips as he continued to suck and bite, until every last shudder was spent.

When he inched his way up to lie beside her, he relished the dreamy look in her eyes. She lay next to him, clearly sated.

She whispered, "I love you."

Wyatt had never known that three little words could sound so wonderful. It tightened his heart, knotted his throat. "Do you?" he teased, attempting to brush away the strong emotion.

She cocked a brow. With her palm she firmly pushed him onto his back. Then, like a lithe cat she crawled over him, her eyelids half shuttered. She looked so sexy, so sensual as she straddled him. Her hips rose, taking his hard erection into her body.

"Talented," he chuckled.

"Yeah, and now I'm going to show you just how *much* I love you." She swayed, working her hips, moving her body, her breasts thrusting back and forth as she rode him.

"Ride 'em hard and leave 'em wet," he hummed, joining her in the rhythm as his hips rose to met hers.

"You bet, cowboy, forever and ever."

"Mmmm...I like the sound of forever." Now that he had found Lacy, he was never going to let her go.

Why an electronic book?

We live in the Information Age—an exciting time in the history of human civilization, in which technology rules supreme and continues to progress in leaps and bounds every minute of every day. For a multitude of reasons, more and more avid literary fans are opting to purchase e-books instead of paper books. The question from those not yet initiated into the world of electronic reading is simply: *Why?*

1. ***Price.*** An electronic title at Ellora's Cave Publishing and Cerridwen Press runs anywhere from 40% to 75% less than the cover price of the exact same title in paperback format. Why? Basic mathematics and cost. It is less expensive to publish an e-book (no paper and printing, no warehousing and shipping) than it is to publish a paperback, so the savings are passed along to the consumer.

2. ***Space.*** Running out of room in your house for your books? That is one worry you will never have with electronic books. For a low one-time cost, you can purchase a handheld device specifically designed for e-reading. Many e-readers have large, convenient screens for viewing. Better yet, hundreds of titles can be stored within your new library—on a single microchip. There are a variety of e-readers from different manufacturers. You can also read e-books on your PC or laptop computer. (Please note that Ellora's Cave does not endorse any specific brands.

You can check our websites at www.ellorascave.com or www.cerridwenpress.com for information we make available to new consumers.)

3. *Mobility.* Because your new e-library consists of only a microchip within a small, easily transportable e-reader, your entire cache of books can be taken with you wherever you go.

4. *Personal Viewing Preferences.* Are the words you are currently reading too small? Too large? Too… ANNOYING? Paperback books cannot be modified according to personal preferences, but e-books can.

5. *Instant Gratification.* Is it the middle of the night and all the bookstores near you are closed? Are you tired of waiting days, sometimes weeks, for bookstores to ship the novels you bought? Ellora's Cave Publishing sells instantaneous downloads twenty-four hours a day, seven days a week, every day of the year. Our webstore is never closed. Our e-book delivery system is 100% automated, meaning your order is filled as soon as you pay for it.

Those are a few of the top reasons why electronic books are replacing paperbacks for many avid readers.

As always, Ellora's Cave and Cerridwen Press welcome your questions and comments. We invite you to email us at Comments@ellorascave.com or write to us directly at Ellora's Cave Publishing Inc., 1056 Home Avenue, Akron, OH 44310-3502.

Cerridwen, the Celtic Goddess of wisdom, was the muse who brought inspiration to storytellers and those in the creative arts. Cerridwen Press encompasses the best and most innovative stories in all genres of today's fiction. Visit our site and discover the newest titles by talented authors who still get inspired - much like the ancient storytellers did, once upon a time.